Fit to Be Tied

Before Fargo could strain against the ropes over his wrists, Sutton grabbed his arms and gave them a yank. He moved Fargo's hands back and forth. "It's a bit loose."

Garson snickered. "Retie the knots, and add another rope for insurance." He smiled at Fargo. "Hope you don't hold it against me."

Fargo spat. "Go to hell."

Once Sutton was done, Garson tested the ropes himself. "Good job, Billy."

Sutton puffed out his chest. "Anything you want, just give the word, Mr. Garson. Thanks to you, we'll all be rolling in gold soon."

"You're mad," Fargo growled.

"Yes, sir," Tuck Garson said to no one in particular. "Tomorrow it starts. Months and months of planning will be put to the test. We're about to do what no one else has ever done, boys. We're going to lock horns with the U.S. government." Garson's eyes widened with insanity. "And by the time we're through, the plains will run red with blood."

THE
TRAILSMAN
#228

WYOMING
WAR CRY

by

Jon Sharpe

A SIGNET BOOK

SIGNET
Published by New American Library, a division of
Penguin Putnam Inc., 375 Hudson Street,
New York, New York 10014, U.S.A.
Penguin Books Ltd, 27 Wrights Lane,
London W8 5TZ, England
Penguin Books Australia Ltd, Ringwood,
Victoria, Australia
Penguin Books Canada Ltd, 10 Alcorn Avenue,
Toronto, Ontario, Canada M4V 3B2
Penguin Books (N.Z.) Ltd, 182–190 Wairau Road,
Auckland 10, New Zealand

Penguin Books Ltd, Registered Offices:
Harmondsworth, Middlesex, England

First published by Signet, an imprint of New American Library,
a division of Penguin Putnam Inc.

First Printing, October 2000
10 9 8 7 6 5 4 3 2 1

The Trailsman

Beginnings . . . they bend the tree and they mark the man. Skye Fargo was born when he was eighteen. Terror was his midwife, vengeance his first cry. Killing spawned Skye Fargo, ruthless, cold-blooded murder. Out of the acrid smoke of gunpowder still hanging in the air, he rose, cried out a promise never forgotten.

The Trailsman they began to call him all across the West: searcher, scout, hunter, the man who could see where others only looked, his skills for hire but not his soul, the man who lived each day to the fullest, yet trailed each tomorrow. Skye Fargo, the Trailsman, the seeker who could take the wildness of a land and the wanting of a woman and make them his own.

*Wyoming, 1861—where greed and savagery
run rampant, and the prairie runs red
with the blood of innocents. . . .*

1

The tall rider in buckskins reined up on a low rise and surveyed the prairie ahead. The trail he was following featured something new: a squat building of sod and wood that boasted a rickety corral and a water trough. The rider's lake-blue eyes narrowed, taking in a trio of dusty horses tied to a long hitch rail, and a crudely painted sign that read: HONEST JACK'S TRADE AND LIQUOR EMPORIUM.

Skye Fargo had half a mind to avoid the hovel. He had seen countless others like it in his travels. Dens of iniquity, a parson would brand them, full of sundry two-legged sidewinders better left alone. But Fargo had never minded a little iniquity now and then, and the presence of four wagons parked out front sparked his curiosity. Lightly touching his spurs to his pinto stallion, he trotted on down the rise and over to the rail.

Nearby was a covered wagon. Not a full-size Conestoga, but a smaller model, about half as big, and from what Fargo could tell, crammed with various tools. The other three wagons were actually vans, similar to those the army used to transport the wounded, only these had the words WESTERN UNION TELEGRAPH COMPANY stenciled on their sides.

Dismounting, Fargo looped the Ovaro's reins around the rail and moved toward the door. As he did, a short figure came bustling around the last van and nearly collided with him.

"Hey! Watch where you're going, you big ox!"

Fargo looked down into a dirt-streaked face framed

by a floppy brown hat that covered close-cropped black hair. A baggy shirt and even baggier pants hung in folds on a bony youth who wasn't more than eighteen or nineteen, and didn't stand much over five feet in height. Dark eyes flared with resentment, and small hands balled into fists.

"The least you could do is apologize, mister. What is it with you frontier clods? There isn't one of you who has the manners of a goat." Although the youth didn't have a whisker on his chin, his voice was low and deep. Uncommonly so, Fargo thought. "I have half a mind to thrash you."

Fargo laughed out loud. He couldn't help himself. The chances of that happening were about the same as a buffalo sprouting wings and flying. "Simmer down, runt. You're the one who almost bumped into me."

"Is that a fact?" Bristling, the youth cocked a fist as if he fully intended to throw a punch.

"And as far as manners go," Fargo said good-naturedly, "it's a case of the pot calling the kettle black."

The youth's mouth fell. "Why, you son of a—!" he blurted, and started to swing, but just then someone flew past Fargo and grabbed the hothead's arm.

"Wood Carrington! What in the world do you think you're doing? Get a grip on that temper of yours! You're liable to cost us our jobs."

The newcomer was barely a year older than the first youth, and wore nearly identical clothes—the same sort of floppy hat, the same exceptionally baggy shirt and britches. His face was also splashed with grime, but his eyes were green, not brown, and he averted his face from Fargo's glance. "Sorry, mister. Pay my brother no mind."

"Wood?" Fargo repeated. "Is that his name or what he has between his ears?"

"Damn you!" Wood spat, and would have torn into Fargo if not for his older brother, who pushed him back against the van. "Let go of me, Darr! We can't let ruffians like him talk to us like that!"

"Yes, we can," Darr said. Gripping Wood by both shoulders, Darr shook him as a parent might a misbehaving child. "Listen to me! We have to accept some changes. We're not east of the Mississippi anymore."

"No man can talk to me like that and walk away standing!" Wood huffed.

"Things aren't what they used to be, remember? We have to deal with them on their terms, not ours."

Fargo thought he understood and added his two bits. "Your brother has a point. Out here there are men who will shoot you if you so much as look at them crosswise. Never start a fight you can't finish."

"Better yet," Darr said to his sibling, "never start a fight, period. We can't afford the grief it would bring down on our heads. Understand?"

Wood, sulking, nodded.

"That's a good idea," Fargo complimented Darr, "especially if you're not going to go around heeled." Neither of the youths wore revolvers. Or, for that matter, carried any weapons whatsoever. "Maybe you should buy yourselves a couple of knives."

"No need," Darr said, releasing his brother. "Some of the men in our party have guns. They'll protect us if we run into danger."

"Your party?" Fargo glanced at the van. "The two of you work for the telegraph company?"

"We string line for them, yes." Darr began to smooth his rumpled shirt, then, oddly, jerked his hands down. "We're to help push the telegraph clear to California by the end of the year, if not sooner. In case civil war breaks out."

"Do tell," Fargo said. He'd heard rumors war was imminent but nothing about the telegraph.

"Don't you read the newspapers?" Wood asked sarcastically.

"Behave," Darr said.

Wood ignored his brother. "Our country is growing by leaps and bounds, mister. Thirty-one million, that's how many people we have now. Pretty soon there won't be room for bumpkins like you."

"Oh, there's plenty of room," Fargo said. He should know. His wide-flung gallivanting had taken him from Canada to Mexico, from the muddy Mississippi to the far-off Pacific coast. Few Easterners truly appreciated how vast the country was, and how much of it had yet to be explored, much less settled.

"In twenty years there won't be," Wood crowed. "People will come flocking west, and before you know it, there will be as many towns and cities as there are back East. The days of the redskin and uncouth louts like you are numbered."

In that, Fargo reflected, the youth might well be right. The California gold rush and the boom of emigrants along the Oregon Trail were proof the States were bursting at the seams. But where Wood saw the exodus as progress, Fargo saw it as a plague of locusts about to sweep over the land, devouring everything in their path.

Darr was speaking. "Again, I apologize for my brother, mister. He's always been rather opinionated."

"Bullheaded, is more like it," Fargo said. "Keep a tight rein on him, or one of these days his opinions will be the death of him."

Wood stiffened. "Was that a threat?"

Fargo was tired of the boy's antics. "No, a prediction." Wheeling, Fargo strode indoors, stopping just inside so his eyes could adjust to the gloom, and his nose to the stink.

The Emporium reeked of must and sweat and whiskey and other odors better left unidentified. To the left was the dry-goods section, four measly shelves stacked with barely enough housewares to fill a cupboard. To the right were several tables and a long plank bar. Behind it, neatly arranged, were enough liquor bottles to satisfy the needs of the entire Sixth Cavalry.

The proprietor, Honest Jack, was a portly fellow with a belly as big as a stove and a head as bald as marble. He wore shabby clothes and an apron that hadn't been cleaned since the turn of the century. Smiling broadly, he beckoned and said, "Howdy, stranger. What's your poison?"

Fargo ambled over, aware that three grungy characters at a corner table were taking his measure. He returned the favor. One was a hulking brute in a heavy buffalo-hide coat, the other a swarthy breed with a nasty scar on his cheek, and the third a pasty-faced weasel who wore two guns, strapped low.

The other patrons, seven men lining the bar, Fargo rated as no threat. They were drinking and laughing and joking. Western Union workers, Fargo guessed. Angling past them to the end of the plank, he stood so a wall was behind him. Old habits were hard to break.

The barkeep ambled over. "You still haven't said what you'd like, stranger. I've got it all. Whiskey, scotch, bourbon, rum. Hell, I even have a bottle of wine for those with sissified taste."

"Coffin varnish will do me fine," Fargo said.

"One whiskey, coming right up."

The door opened and shafts of sunlight speared the floorboards. In walked Darr and Wood, their hat brims pulled low. They moved to a table near Fargo and sat with their backs to the others.

A gray-haired character at the bar shifted toward them. He had chipmunk cheeks, a bulbous nose, and a kindly expression. "Don't you boys care to partake? It'll be a spell before we get to drink again."

"Not until we reach Fort Laramie," added a spindly individual at his side, a scarecrow in homespun with an Adam's apple the size of a melon.

"No, thank you, Mr. Melton," Darr told the kindly old-timer. "We don't fancy hard drink all that much."

"Are you addlepated?" Melton joked. "Liquor is God's gift to all us fools and sinners."

"Not only that," the scarecrow added, "it puts hair on a fella's chest."

"How would you know, Charlie?" Melton said. "Your chest is as bare as a baby's bottom."

At that, the entire telegraph crew cackled.

Only Fargo saw the three men at the corner table exchange glances. And he was the only one who saw the weasel in the black hat and vest rise and strut toward the brothers, thumbs hooked in his gunbelt. As casually as could be, Fargo lowered his right hand to his side.

"So you two boys don't like to drink?" the weasel declared, dripping with scorn. "Where are you brats from, anyhow, that they don't teach you proper?"

Darr and Wood looked up. "Keep your ugly nose out of our business, mister," the latter answered.

The two-gun man stopped cold. "Better watch that mouth of yours, sonny, or you'll bite off more than you can chew."

Darr came to his brother's defense again. "He didn't mean no insult. Don't hold it against him."

Melton took a step toward their table but froze when the hardcase in the black vest dropped a hand to a polished gun butt. "They're just boys, friend. Fresh off the farm. They don't know any better."

From the table in the corner came a hearty guffaw, a slow, mocking laugh from the barrel chest of the hulking brute in the buffalo coat. "You hear that, Brody? Green as grass. Maybe the sprouts need to be clipped down to size."

"I hear, Angus. I hear," Brody said, sneering at the youths.

Melton and the Western Union men at the bar swapped worried looks. Melton stepped toward the gunman, smiling to show his intentions were friendly. "Listen, mister. We're not looking for trouble. We're on our way to Fort Laramie, and from there we'll be helping extend the telegraph line west."

"Is that a fact?" Brody said.

Melton moved between the hardcase and the table. "We've been on the go all day and we're bushed. I thought it would be nice to have a couple of drinks before we make camp for the night. I'm in charge of this crew."

"Who gives a damn?"

The foreman was no fool. Nervously licking his lips, he tried once more to make peace. "We'll be on our way, if it's all right with you. There's still another hour or so of daylight left, and it would be a shame to waste it." Melton gestured at the men at the bar and at the two brothers, motioning for them to get out of there.

Brody's hand shot out, lightning quick, gripping Melton by the shirt. "You'll leave when I say you can leave and not before, you old geezer."

Fargo looked at the proprietor, who showed no interest in intervening. Honest Jack had brought a glass over and was pouring three fingers of whiskey. "You're not going to do anything?" Fargo asked quietly so no one else would overhear.

"Are you loco?" Honest Jack whispered. "Buck Frank Brody? I might as well bait a wolverine in its den. He's snake mean, mister." Jack leaned forward. "Him and his partners, Angus Stark and Pawnee Tom, have been hanging around for days now, making my life miserable. They picked on a drummer yesterday. Made the poor cuss eat a pair of socks he was selling. The guy about choked to death."

Brody had pushed Melton aside and was glaring at the brothers. "What will it be, brats? You can eat crow or you can be carried out of here."

Darr began to rise but stopped when Brody tensed as if to draw. "Look, this is ridiculous. Why can't we handle this like adults?"

Angus Stark's hearty mirth rose to the rafters. "He's callin' you immature, Brody. Sayin' you're more of a kid than he is."

"Is that so?" The gunman strutted nearer, his spurs jangling.

"I said no such thing," Darr responded, shoving himself erect. "And I'll be darned if we're going to sit here and be made laughingstocks." He tugged at his brother's sleeve but Wood wouldn't budge.

"You'll be *darned,* huh?" Brody said, mimicking the younger man's tone and inflection. "Mercy me, but you brats sure do use hard language."

Angus and Pawnee Tom roared with laughter but no

one else joined in. Frank Brody, cocky as a bantam rooster, swaggered right up to their table. "Maybe I should wash both your mouths out with soap."

Wood snapped. Beet red with anger, he came up out of his chair and jabbed a finger at Brody. "I'd like to see you try, you uppity wretch! You would be in for the shock of your worthless life."

Brody's mouth became a thin slit. "I would, would I?" He sidled to the left so he was facing them. "You're the one in for a shock, mealy mouth. Get down on your knees and beg me to spare you or I'll pistol-whip you within an inch of your life."

"I'd die first!" Wood said.

"Hush, will you?" Darr beseeched his kin, then sank onto a knee, facing Brody. "How about if I do it instead? Here, I'm begging for our lives. I'm pleading with you to let us go our way in peace."

"You don't sound sincere enough," Brody said.

Fargo had witnessed enough. Pivoting so his left elbow was on the counter and his right hand was brushing his Colt, he said calmly, "That's enough fun for one day. Let the boys be."

Brody had the posture of a rattler about to strike. He flicked Fargo a look of annoyance and rasped, "This doesn't concern you, mister."

"I say it does."

Angus and Pawnee Tom stood and crossed toward their companion, Angus cradling a Sharps in the crook of his left elbow, Pawnee Tom fingering the hilt of a Bowie in a beaded-leather sheath on his right hip. The half-breed wore buckskin leggins and knee-high moccasins, also elaborately beaded.

"I pegged you as a busybody the second I saw you," the big buffalo hunter addressed Fargo. "Some folks just don't know when to leave well enough alone."

At long last Honest Jack spoke up. "Now, hold on there, fellas. I don't cotton to gunplay in my establishment. Something is bound to get busted, and my liquor and trade goods don't grow on trees."

"Shut up, you spineless yack," Angus said.

"Yes, sir," Honest Jack bleated.

Fargo focused on Frank Brody. When the violence erupted, Brody would make the first move. Fargo had met others like him, cocky coyotes who acted as if they owned the world, cruel bastards who took great delight in causing others pain and misery. "I'll only say this once. Leave now, and no one need be hurt."

Angus snorted. "Damned generous of you, mister, considering we outnumber you three to one."

"He's bluffing," Brody said. "Ain't no way in hell he can take all of us. Not all of us, he can't."

Darr was still on one knee. Abruptly standing, he went to move between Fargo and the gunman. "You gentlemen can't be serious! You wouldn't really shoot one another over such a trifle, would you? That would be barbaric."

Angus gave the youth a shove that flung Darr onto the table. Darr would have tumbled off the other side had Wood not caught hold of him.

"Keep out of this, boy," the buffalo hunter snapped.

Pawnee Tom was craftily edging to the left so he would have a clear throw. He stopped when Fargo glanced at him.

Frank Brody's mouth creased in an arrogant smirk. "So how should we go about it, Angus? Do we let the breed whittle this jasper down to size with his pigsticker, or should I do the honors?" Brody chuckled, the sound like flint grating on steel. "I think it should be me. I ain't shot anyone in pretty near a month."

Fargo didn't bother replying. He had said his piece. Now the outcome was up to the three cutthroats. They would get to it eventually. Just as four-legged wolves sometimes had to work themselves into a killing frenzy before attacking moose or elk, the two-legged variety often needed to bolster their own backbone with boasts and threats.

The scarecrow at the bar, Charlie, slapped down his glass and rotated toward the entrance. "Enough of this! Let's head out before one of us takes a slug by mistake."

Brody glowered at him. "String bean, if you take a

bullet, it won't be by accident. I'll shoot you plumb between the eyes if you so much as take a step."

Gulping, Charlie transformed into a statue. "Western Union warned us about savages and wild critters and the elements. But they never said anything about situations like this."

The big buffalo hunter chuckled. "Where in hell do you reckon you are, pilgrim? New York City? Out here a gent can cut his throat with his own tongue if he ain't powerful careful."

"It's silly," Darr said.

"It's stupid," was Wood's opinion.

"It's how things are," Brody corrected them both, and just like that, while everyone was distracted by their chatter, he went for his pistols, his hands swooping down and palming the matched set of nickel-plated Remingtons. He thought his ruse had worked. He thought he had Fargo dead to rights, and as he leveled the revolvers, he grinned.

Pawnee Tom was grinning, too, as his right hand flashed to his Bowie and he whipped the knife in an overhand throw.

Fargo exploded into motion, the Colt materializing as if it had leaped into his hand of its own accord. It boomed once, and Frank Brody tottered. It boomed twice, and the gunman was slammed backward as if smashed by an invisible fist and became entangled with a chair.

As the bantam gunny toppled, Fargo pivoted. Pawnee Tom's arm was at the apex of its swing. Another instant, and he would release the Bowie.

Fargo fanned the Colt, a trick he seldom resorted to unless at close range and he needed to get off a shot quickly.

Two swift blasts raised Pawnee Tom onto the tips of his toes. Like melted wax oozing down a candle, the half-breed seeped to the floor in a heap.

Fargo swung the Colt toward the buffalo hunter and thumbed back the hammer. The click was unnaturally loud in the sudden stillness. "How about you?"

Angus Stark hadn't so much as twitched a muscle. Tearing his eyes from his fallen friends, he grinned at the wisps of smoke curling from the muzzle of Fargo's six-shooter. "Whooee! That was some shootin', mister. I ain't seen the like in all my born days."

"You can see it again if you want," Fargo said.

"No, sir. Not here. Not now." With exaggerated slowness, the buffalo hunter laid the big Sharps down on a table and stepped back with his calloused hands in the air. "My momma didn't raise no simpletons."

Melton and the rest of the Western Union crew were flabbergasted. Charlie's mouth, in particular, was parted wide enough to admit a swarm of flies.

Darr was gawking at the prone forms in disbelief, but Wood was beaming like a kid just given a hatful of hard candy. "Serves them right!" he exclaimed.

Honest Jack came around the end of the bar, his eyes as large as saucers. "They're getting blood all over my floor!" he complained, then scanned the room and cheered up considerably. "Nothing was busted, though. How about that! Miracles do happen."

Darr tore his gaze from the spreading scarlet pool. "Is everyone in this godforsaken land insane? Come on." He seized Wood by the arm and hauled him toward the door. "We're getting out of here."

Wood glanced at Fargo and silently mouthed, "Thank you."

The door slammed in their wake, rousing the other workmen. Melton fumbled in a pocket and slapped change on the counter. "We're leaving, too! I never should have stopped in the first place."

Within moments Fargo was alone with the buffalo hunter and the owner. Still covering Angus, Fargo polished off his drink, fished in his own pocket for some money, and paid Honest Jack. Then he backed out, snagging the Sharps along the way. "I'll leave this at the end of the corral. But don't get any ideas."

"Don't look at me," Stark said. "I'm not hankerin' to be turned into a sieve if I can help it."

Honest Jack was checking the pulses of the fallen. "The breed is dead, but Brody still has a heartbeat." He looked up. "What do you want me to do with him?"

"Bury him alive for all I care," Fargo answered. Pushing the door open with his shoulder, he peeked outside before committing himself. The covered wagon and the vans were lumbering into motion, the drivers cracking whips to goad their teams.

Darr and Wood were on the last van. Wood caught sight of Fargo in the doorway and gave a little wave.

"Hold that open for me, will you?" Honest Jack hollered as he commenced dragging the body of Pawnee Tom. To Angus Stark, he said, "I'll be back in just a minute to help doctor our friend."

"No hurry," the hunter said, as if Brody's life meant nothing to him.

Fargo propped the door with his foot until the owner had shambled past. Letting it close, he stepped toward the Ovaro, never taking his eyes off the burlap-covered window.

"Pssst! Hold on, hombre!" Honest Jack whispered. "There's something you should know." Dropping Pawnee Tom with a thud, he scurried over. "What you did wasn't too bright. You're new to these parts so maybe you haven't heard."

"Heard what?"

"About Tuck Garson and his pack of killers. Folks say Garson's favorite pastime is to stake out people he doesn't like and skin them alive."

Tales of Garson's brutal exploits had been spreading like wildfire across the frontier. It was claimed the man was more animal than human. "So what does that have to do with me?" Fargo asked.

"Well, I can't prove it, mind you, but I've suspected for some time that Angus, Brody and Pawnee Tom were part of Tuck Garson's outfit." Honest Jack paused to let the full import sink in. "I hope to heaven I'm wrong, mister. Because if I'm not, the most vicious bunch of curly wolves this side of creation are going to be after your hide."

2

Skye Fargo did as he had promised and left the big Sharps propped against the rickety corral. He had a feeling he might regret it later. But since the buffalo hunter hadn't tried to harm him, since Angus had, in fact, stood there smirking when the other two were gunned down, Fargo couldn't bring himself to break it or take it.

On the frontier there were two things a man never did. One was to steal a horse. Rustling was a capital offense, and the inevitable result was a necktie social. The other taboo was to take a man's gun unless given ample cause. Rifles and revolvers were as essential to survival as a good mount. When a person had theirs taken, they usually hunted up a new one, then tracked the culprit down and expressed their displeasure with hot lead.

So Fargo rode westward, glancing back often to insure the buffalo hunter didn't reclaim the Sharps and try to backshoot him. Angus Stark never emerged, though, and soon Fargo was out of sight of Honest Jack's.

A stone's throw ahead, clattering noisily and spewing dust from under their wheels, were the covered wagon and the vans.

Fargo intended to go on by and continue on to Fort Laramie. An acquaintance of his, a major by the name of Canby, had sent for him, asking that he get there as soon as possible.

Overtaking the last van, Fargo swung wide and brought the Ovaro to a trot. As he passed, Darr saw him and nodded. Wood grinned, giving the same odd little wave.

Fargo touched the brim of his hat. Fish out of water, he thought. If they weren't more careful in the future, they'd never make it back to the States, never again see that farm they were from. They had to learn right quick that west of the Mississippi there was hardly any law but an abundance of lawbreakers. In order to survive, a man had to keep as tight a rein on his mouth as he did on his mount.

The pinto trotted by the other vans and started to pull ahead of the covered wagon. Melton and Charlie were in the seat, Charlie handling the team. Melton looked around in surprise, then smiled and cupped a hand to his mouth. "Hold on there, friend! Where are you bound, if I might ask?"

Slowing, Fargo told him.

"In that case, I've got a proposition for you. Do you mind making camp with us tonight? We'll be stopping pretty soon."

Fargo had planned to push on until well past dark. "I don't think—" he began.

"We'll make it worth your while," the old man said. "We have a fresh side of beef, and I bought a couple of bottles of conversation fluid back yonder. You're more than welcome to share."

Charlie, flicking his whip, threw in, "And I'm a damned good cook, if I do say so myself."

All Fargo had was a few beans. He had been living off the land for over a week and was tired of rabbit and squirrel stew. Deer were plentiful, but he was reluctant to kill a buck or doe when most of the meat would go to waste, since he couldn't take the time to make jerky or pemmican.

"What do you say, friend?" Melton urged.

"I'd say you have a dinner guest," Fargo quipped.

Toward twilight, the telegraph crew called a halt in a clearing along the North Platte River. All the usual precautions were taken; the wagons were arranged in a

14

circle, the horses tethered in a string. A tripod was set up over the fire and coffee was set on to boil. Charlie rigged a spit and impaled a large chunk of meat, which he hovered over with the diligence of a hawk over a chicken coop.

Fargo was left to himself for a while. He hobbled the Ovaro, spread out his bedroll, and hunkered by the fire, his Henry beside him. The workers, he noticed, were a bit edgy around him, understandable in light of what they had witnessed.

At length Melton sank down with a contented sigh and declared, "Done for the day at last! All that's left is to eat and turn in. Well, and drink some." Chortling, he opened a large leather bag and took out a bottle of cheap whiskey.

The others drifted over. Darr and Wood sat across from Fargo but well back from the fire, their faces in shadow.

Charlie repeatedly turned the spit and poked the beef with a butcher knife. "It won't be long," he announced grandly, "before we're feasting on prime beef."

"Prime elk, you mean," Fargo corrected him.

Melton, in the act of opening the bottle, looked up. "Eh? You're mistaken."

"No, I'm not." The texture and the aroma had tipped Fargo off. "It's elk meat," he reiterated. "Old elk meat, at that."

"It can't be!" Charlie declared, lowering his nose to the spit and sniffing loudly. "Honest Jack told us it was real beef from a cow he took in trade."

"Did you ever see the cow's hide?" Fargo asked.

"But why would he trick us?" Charlie said.

"Simple. Beef sells for five times as much as elk. So whenever anyone stops by, he just happens to mention that he has a side of beef for sale."

Charlie wagged the knife as if it were a sword. "That mangy son of a bitch! I have half a mind to go and demand our money back. We paid top dollar."

"We can't afford another day's delay," Melton said.

"Besides, elk meat is better than no meat at all. And we're not much at hunting." He enjoyed a healthy swig, then wiped his mouth with his sleeve and handed the bottle to Fargo. "Treat yourself, friend."

From his saddlebags Fargo took a battered tin cup and filled it half full. "I'm obliged," he said, relaying the bottle to the next man. "Now, what's this proposition you mentioned earlier?"

"We'd like you to ride with us to Fort Laramie." Melton got right to it. "Sort of escort us, like a scout with a wagon train."

"I was hoping to get there sooner," Fargo mentioned.

"What can another couple of days hurt?" Melton said. "We'll push as hard as we can. It would help all of us sleep a whole lot easier knowing we had someone with your savvy watching over us. Especially after what happened today."

From across the fire, Darr cleared his throat. "Won't a lawman come looking for you, mister?"

"No," Fargo answered. "A territorial marshal hasn't been appointed yet. And even if there was one, he'd have thousands of square miles to cover. He couldn't be bothered over a minor shooting scrape."

"Why in blazes not?" Wood asked. "Or do folks out here gun each other down and no one gives a hoot?"

"Please, boy," Melton said. "Don't be insulting."

"What about the military?" Darr asked.

"The army doesn't involve itself in civilian affairs," Fargo said.

"But two men were killed."

"Just one," Fargo mentioned. "Frank Brody was alive when I left."

"Don't quibble," Darr bickered. "You still shot down two human beings. And while I know you were only trying to help us, I wish there had been some other way."

"There wasn't," Fargo stated.

"You could have tried to reason with them," Wood said.

Fargo would only abide so much ignorance. "Can you reason with rabid dogs?" he countered. "Or mad grizzlies? Men like Brody and Pawnee Tom are no different. They kill for the sheer hell of it."

"No one can be that mean," Wood disagreed.

Fargo stared at the youths a moment, then sadly shook his head. "You two have no business being here. You're like calves being led to the slaughter."

Melton had his hands on the bottle again. "Pay them no mind. They're young, is all. They haven't learned the wicked ways of the world."

"And they never will if they go around with blinders on," Fargo said. He had to remind himself that he had been on the frontier for so long, he had forgotten there were people who went their entire lives without seeing another person killed, people who lived from cradle to grave in comfort and security, people who took it for granted that since they couldn't harm a fly, no one else would either.

"We're fast learners, mister," Darr said belligerently.

"You'd better be," Fargo replied. "Out here are few second chances. If you're not going to go around heeled, then at least keep your mouths shut when men like Brody are on the prod."

"Say," Melton changed the subject, "it just hit me. You haven't told us your name yet, friend. Mind my asking?"

Fargo revealed who he was.

A sly smile curled the older man's mouth. "I figured as much. I saw you once, in Springfield, Missouri. That time you had the shooting match with Dottie Wheatridge and Vin Chadwell. Remember?"

Fargo would never forget. The match had been rigged, and he had nearly lost his life to the crooked promoter.

"Land sakes, that was some exhibition!" Melton exclaimed. "Finest shooting I ever did see. You had the highest score, as I recollect. It was a shame the judges disqualified you when you ran off, but how were they to know you were trying to stop that Quigby fella from stealing the receipts?"

"Are you telling us Mr. Fargo is famous?" Wood inquired.

"Famous enough," Melton said.

Now it was Fargo who wanted to change the subject. "Tell me more about the plans to push the telegraph line west."

"There's not much *to* tell," Melton said. "You've heard all the talk about war in the wind? Well, the president wants California and Oregon linked up with the rest of the country before that happens. So Western Union is sending every worker they can spare. I'm from Joplin. The brothers, there, are from Ohio. Charlie is from Illinois." He paused. "You get the idea. We were ordered to the Kansas City office, where the company outfitted us and told us to report to Fort Laramie."

"The telegraph line is just the first step," one of the other men remarked. "Pushing the railroad through will be next. By the end of the decade, the newspapers say."

"Won't that be great?" Charlie said.

Fargo didn't think so. New hordes would push west. New towns and cities would spring up. Before long the prairie would fall to the plow and the mountains would be overrun. It would be the end of an era, an end to the way of life he loved. The prospect was too depressing to contemplate.

"The Indians aren't going to like it, though," Melton predicted. "Another reason I'd like you to escort us is that Honest Jack told us there are hostiles in these parts."

"This is Indian country," Fargo noted. "The Sioux are to the northeast. To the northwest are the Cheyenne, the Arapaho to the southwest. Southeast of here are the Pawnees. And the Shoshones come out of the mountains from time to time to hunt buffalo."

"It's the Sioux that worry me most. They've been acting up of late, committing all kinds of atrocities."

"Whites have committed their share as well," Fargo said.

"Maybe so. But I've never mistreated Indians, and I don't aim to be scalped by them for something I've never done. So will you do it? Will you ride with us to the post?"

Fargo hesitated. They were in little danger. The odds of the Sioux straying that far south were slim. "I'll sleep on it and let you know in the morning," he hedged.

Charlie sliced off a strip of meat and bit into it. "Right tasty," he declared. "Give it another five minutes and supper will be ready."

Melton patted the bottle. "I've got all the supper I need right here."

The others chuckled, but their merry mood was short-lived.

"I'm curious, Mr. Fargo. How many men have you killed?" Wood asked. The group fell silent.

"None of your damn business."

The resentment in Fargo's tone caused the brothers to sit up, and Wood to say, "No need to bite my head off. I was just curious."

Melton answered before Fargo could. "Hellfire, boy. Haven't you heard what curiosity did to the cat? Out here, you can't go nosing into someone else's past. Out here, a person's business is their own."

Wood snorted. "Out here this, out there that. You make it sound as if we're in a whole new world."

"You are," Fargo said bluntly. "A world where all the rules you've lived by no longer apply. A world where only the strong survive."

"Surely you exaggerate," Darr said. "It can't be as bad as all that or no one would ever set foot out of the States."

"You'll learn for yourself soon enough," Fargo said. Everyone did, sooner or later. The trail west was strewn with the bleached bones of those who took the wilderness too lightly, those who paid for their folly with their lives.

"Enough of this grim talk," Melton aid. "Let's jaw about something else. Did any of you hear about the world boxing championship?" He swallowed back more bug juice. "Heenan and Sayers fought for over two hours. The officials finally had to break it up after thirty-six rounds because the crowd got too rowdy."

The conversation drifted to politics. Soon Charlie handed Fargo a tin plate heaped high with simmering elk meat, seasoned with wild onions and salt. Fargo hungrily dug in. His back against his saddle, he watched a multitude of stars blossom like sparkling flowers and listened to the distant yip of wandering coyotes.

Along about ten, the tired men turned in. Fargo stayed up, though, treating himself to his fifth cup of coffee. The night was peaceful. Upriver a bullfrog croaked, while in the trees that lined the river an owl was asking the question all owls asked.

Fargo upended the cup, smacked his lips, and slid under his blankets. The scarecrow was snoring loud enough to be mistaken for a steam engine. Hoping it wouldn't keep him awake, Fargo started to roll onto his side.

A series of faint thuds gave Fargo second thoughts. Sitting up, he heard them grow louder. They were hoof-beats. A horse was riding hard from the east, from the direction of Honest Jack's Emporium. For a lone rider to be abroad so late at night was unusual.

Flinging the blankets off, Fargo grabbed the Henry and rose. He hastily removed his spurs, then padded between two vans and over to the trail. Calling it a road would be more appropriate. Ten to twelve feet wide, it was laced with deep ruts and tramped bare by countless feet.

Gazing eastward, Fargo heard the rider slow, the horse advancing at a walk until it was just beyond the nearest bend. Then the rider reined up.

Fargo sidestepped to some cottonwoods and squatted. Whoever was out there had spotted the glow from their dying fire. He waited for the hoofbeats to resume but they didn't. Which was also unusual.

Gliding from one slender bole to the next, Fargo worked his way toward the bend. Suddenly, off in the undergrowth, a vague shape appeared, flitting from thicket to thicket. The figure was moving toward the river so Fargo did likewise, only to lose sight of the darkling form seconds later.

Stopping, Fargo bent low to the ground so anyone moving about would be silhouetted against the sky. He had a hunch who the mysterious skulker was. Certainly not an Indian, since lone warriors seldom ventured far from their villages after the sun went down. The rider's woodlore, though, rivaled an Indian's, for although Fargo strained his ears to their utmost, he detected no sound.

Then something rustled. But not in front of Fargo, *behind* him. Somehow, the man had slipped past him as silently as a specter and was now close to the wagons and the unsuspecting Western Union crew.

Rotating, Fargo crept through the brush with all the stealth at his command. He probed high and low, right and left, without success, until, without warning, an inky bulk rose directly between him and the smoldering fire. He brought up the Henry but the figure dropped from view.

Worried, Fargo went faster, faster than was prudent, and inadvertently stepped on a dry twig that crunched under his weight. The sound wasn't loud but it must have been loud enough, because the next moment the night was seared by a flash of fire and a clap of thunder, and a slug whistled within inches of Fargo's left ear.

Fargo answered in kind, pumping the Henry's lever, banging off three shots in half as many seconds. He deliberately fired low in order to avoid accidentally hitting any of the telegraph crew. At his third shot, a bearish apparition barreled out of dense growth and off toward the trail.

Veering to cut the man off, Fargo saw the dull glint

21

of a metallic object. Instinctively, he dived flat a heart-beat before a pistol cracked. Rolling to the right, he fixed a bead on a weaving outline and squeezed off an answering round.

The figure never slowed.

Surging upright, heedless of shouts from the camp, Fargo raced in pursuit. The intruder was making a bee-line for the bend and the waiting horse.

Fargo ran flat out. He vaulted a log, avoided a boulder, but he couldn't narrow the gap. Gruff laughter wafted on the breeze. Mocking laughter. Familiar laughter, confirming what Fargo already knew. He came to an open space and whipped the Henry up, but intervening brush spoiled his aim.

"Damn." Fargo ran on. He was forty feet shy of the bend when hooves drummed and the mocking laughter rose to a lusty, wolfish howl. He reached the turn in time to see the rider melt into the night, his heavy buffalo coat flapping like the wings of a giant bat.

"Next time, Stark," Fargo said to himself.

Melton's panicked party were yelling his name over and over. Hurrying back, Fargo called out to identify himself so no one would blister him with bullets.

"What happened?" Charlie inquired, clutching an old Walker Colt. "What was all the ruckus about?"

"Angus Stark paid us a visit," Fargo revealed, striding to the fire and adding a few pieces of wood.

"What was he after?" Melton asked.

"Me." Fargo doubted it would be the last he saw of the wily buffalo hunter. When predators like Stark took it into their heads to make maggot food of someone, they didn't give up until they had done what they set out to do, or were maggot bait themselves. And if Honest Jack was right about Angus being a member of the Garson gang, the next time the buffalo hunter showed up, he might not be alone.

"He's after you for gunning down his pards," Melton said.

"Or for the thrill of it."

Darr and Wood were by their van, partly hidden in shadows. "Only someone who was rotten to the core would get a thrill from killing another human being," the older youth said, his voice a bit more high-pitched than normal in his nervous excitement.

"Which is exactly what I've been trying to tell you," Fargo said. "Stay in the West long enough and you'll meet a lot more just like Stark and Brody."

"Men!" Wood spat in disgust.

"What's that supposed to mean?" Melton said. "There have always been good men and bad men. Remember Cain and Abel? David and Goliath?"

Charlie snickered. "Since when did you become a Bible-thumper, George?"

"Go sit on a porcupine," the old-timer retorted, and plopped down onto his bedding. "Let's all try and catch more shut-eye. That polecat won't be back now that we've run him off."

"Is that true, Mr. Fargo?" Darr asked pensively.

"I doubt he'll bother us again tonight." Which was as far as Fargo would commit himself. He wouldn't put *anything* past a man like Angus Stark, including resorting to the oldest ruse there was: circling around to try again. "The rest of you can turn back in. I'll keep watch."

Everyone did so, the brothers crawling back under their van. Fargo wondered why it was that the pair kept so aloof from the others, why they sat apart and ate apart and slept apart, as if they had something to hide.

Of course, they wouldn't be the first. Many who had come west were fleeing the law or running from one thing or another. Tuck Garson was one of them. Rumor had it he was from Kentucky, that he had been a highwayman until one foggy night when he murdered a man who resisted, and had to head for parts unknown before a posse closed in. Once he reached the frontier, Garson had gone on a robbing and killing spree that renegade Apaches would envy.

A reward had been posted, but so far no one had

been able to claim the bounty. The problem, as Fargo understood it, was that the authorities had no idea what Garson looked like.

Shaking the coffee pot, Fargo verified that some remained and emptied the dregs into his cup. It would help him stay awake.

After a bit, an uneasy sensation came over him, a feeling he was being watched. Fargo scoured the vegetation but saw no one. Raising the cup to his lips, he peered over it and happened to glimpse a pale face pressed to the spokes of the rear wheel of the van the brothers were under. Darr or Wood was spying on him. Amused more than annoyed, Fargo said gruffly, "You should get some rest, boy. Dawn will be here before you know it."

The face disappeared.

For over half an hour Fargo sat by the fire, until it had burned low and the clearing was once again filled with snores. Then, rolling up his bedding and throwing his saddle over his shoulder, Fargo changed positions and moved into deep gloom just beyond the circle of firelight.

It was two o'clock or later when Fargo finally drifted into dreamland. But he wasn't asleep for long. A grunt from the other side of the river jolted him awake and he sat up, every nerve jangling.

The grunt was repeated. Undergrowth crackled as something neared the narrow waterway.

A bear, Fargo guessed. But was it a black bear or a grizzly? The former were fairly harmless unless it was a sow with cubs or an old male that had caught a whiff of their food. Grizzlies were another matter. As fierce as they were unpredictable, grizzlies were the most formidable creatures on the continent. One swipe from one of their enormous paws was enough to disembowel a man or a horse.

Fargo scoured the opposite bank. Out of the murk hove a monster almost as big as one of the wagons. A blunt snout was raised to the sky and sniffed noisily.

Fargo wedged the Henry against his shoulder in anticipation of a rush, but the bear merely dipped its mouth into the water and lapped like a dog. Then, wheeling, it plowed off into the darkness.

Relaxing, Fargo eased back down. The men slumbering a dozen yards away didn't know how lucky they were. Once, several years ago, Fargo had seen a grizzly tear into a troupe of river men encamped on the Missouri. Four had died, three others had been left maimed for life, and the bear got away without a scratch.

Fargo dozed, but fitfully awoke at every noise, no matter how slight. Toward morning he finally fell into a sound sleep, but it seemed he had hardly closed his eyes when a splashing sound brought him to his feet.

Someone—or something—was crossing the river toward them.

3

Skye Fargo swung toward the North Platte and blinked in confusion. He could neither find signs of another bear, nor anyone attempting to ford the river.

Shaking his head to clear lingering cobwebs, Fargo wondered if he had imagined the whole thing. Judging by the eastern horizon, the sun wouldn't rise for another half an hour yet. He debated rekindling the fire, then heard splashing again. It came from downriver. He also thought he heard the low murmur of voices.

Perplexed, Fargo circled the clearing, counting heads. Everyone was accounted for, the men sleeping as peacefully as babies. Or almost everyone. For when he peeked under the van, he found that Darr and Wood were missing.

As silently as a Comanche, Fargo melted into the woods and paralleled the gurgling North Platte until he came to a grassy mound. On the other side someone giggled, and more water splashed. Easing onto his hands and knees, Fargo crabbed toward the top.

"Hush, consarn it! One of them might hear you. I would hate to be found out now, after coming so far."

"You're a regular worrywart, you know that? Melton and the others are as dumb as shovels If they haven't caught on yet, they never will."

"I still don't see why you had to have a bath now, of all times."

"It could be because I haven't had one in over a week. It could be because in four days we'll be at Fort Laramie, and we sure as blazes won't be able to take a bath there. And after that, who can say? Charlie was telling me water is scarce between Fort Laramie and Fort Bridger."

The voices were those of Darr and Wood, and yet they were different, more high-pitched and melodious. Downright feminine, Fargo mused, as he stretched out on his belly and peered over the top.

Darr was seated on the bank, fully dressed. A few feet away lay a pile of clothes topped by a floppy hat.

Wood was in the river, shoulder deep. As Fargo looked on, Wood waded onto shore, revealing in a rain of watery drops that there was nothing masculine about him. Or, rather, *her*. Wood was one hundred percent, pure and perfect female. Compact but superbly shaped, she had gently sloping shoulders, alabaster arms, pert, firm breasts about the size of apples, and a marvelously flat stomach. Between exquisite marble thighs was a soft downy thatch that hinted at alluring charms waiting to be discovered. She walked with an enticing, graceful sway, her close-cropped black hair shimmering in the pale light.

"I don't see how you can stand it, Carina," Darr said. "That water must be freezing. My teeth would be chattering like crazy."

"You never could stand cold very well, Carrie," Wood responded, stooping to reclaim her garb.

Fargo grinned to himself. So "Darr," was really Carrie, and "Wood" was really Carina, and they were sisters, not brothers. They were playacting, pretending to be men. To what end, he couldn't guess.

Carina took her sweet time getting dressed, pulling on each garment with distaste. "I don't mind telling you, Carrie, I'm sick and tired of this charade of ours. Wearing these baggy clothes, going around all filthy and slouched over."

"It has to be done."

"And having to talk like we do!" Carina continued to complain. "It hurts, darn it. By the end of the day my throat is so sore I can barely swallow."

"Do you want to quit?" Carrie demanded.

"I didn't say that."

"Then quit your bellyaching. We agreed, remember? We knew it would be rough. We knew what we had to endure, but we decided it was worth it."

"I suppose," Carina said, although she didn't sound entirely convinced. Pulling on her oversized shirt, she buttoned it and loosely stuffed the bottom into her baggy pants. Both nicely concealed the delightful contours of her lush body.

Carrie stood. "Look, it's only for another four or five months. Until we have enough money squirreled away to make our dream come true. Surely you can hold out that long?"

"I'll do my best." Carina jammed the hat on her head and tugged the wide brim low. Then, squatting, she scooped up a handful of dirt, rubbed it in her palms, and applied it to her cheeks, smearing them to further disguise her appearance.

"I know how hard this is," Carrie said, softening. "I know what you're going through. I feel the same. But we can't give up now."

"I said I would do my best," Carina stressed. "Lordy, sometimes you sound just like Pa, the way you carp so." Slumping her shoulders, she adopted a slightly stooped posture and thrust her hands into her pockets. "There. Do I look like a typical lunkheaded member of the opposite sex again?"

Carrie giggled. "You sure do. Except men have more of a dumb look about them."

"How's this?" Carina crossed her eyes and poked the tip of her tongue from the corner of her mouth.

Stifling laughter, Carrie nodded. "That's just right."

Carina sobered and took her hands out. "Say, I've been meaning to ask. What do you think of that Fargo fella?"

Her sister arched an eyebrow. "I thought you didn't like him. You called him a bumpkin, as I recollect."

"I was only doing what a man would do if another

man almost bumped into him. You know how they love to bluster and spat." Carina grinned. "To be honest, he's very easy on the eyes."

"Don't you dare!" Carrie said. "I've heard that tone before. I've seen that look. You're smitten, aren't you?"

"Well, you have to admit I could do worse."

"Damn you and your wanton ways." Carrie gripped Carina's arms and shook her, hard. "Now I know why you needed a cold bath! Learn to control these urges of yours or you'll spoil everything."

Carina chortled. "Listen to you, Sis. You should have some urges, as you call them, now and then. They do wonders for the disposition. And Grandma used to say they improve the complexion."

Carrie stamped a foot. "You are hopeless, you know that? Positively hopeless. If Pa could see how you've turned out, he'd roll over in his grave in shame."

"Don't start," Carina said.

"It's true. You've been boy crazy ever since Harold Scrimmer took you up to the hayloft in his barn. And you were only fourteen."

"I'm nineteen now. Old enough to do as I want, when I want."

"But not *now*."

Carina shrugged free. "Hell, you make me sound like a trollop. I'm no hussy! I don't bed every man I see, do I?"

Carrie gave a start and glanced toward the clearing. "Quiet down! We're being too loud. If we're not careful, we'll wake them."

"See if I care."

The older sister gripped the younger. "Please, Carina. For me. For the sake of our futures. *Please.*"

"Oh, all right. But quit accusing me of having the morals of a streetwalker, or so help me, I'll tear off my clothes in front of the whole crew and your pipe dream will never come true."

"It's *our* dream, I thought," Carrie said quietly.

"Yours and mine, together. I'd never have started this if I knew you were only doing it for my sake."

Carina's lips quirked upward. "That was my temper talking. I want it as much as you do. So don't fret. I might grouse a lot, but I'll see this through to the end. You have my word."

Fargo sensed they were about to head back. Sliding down the mound, he hastened to camp. A pink band rimmed the eastern horizon, but no one else was up yet. Sliding under his blankets, he feigned sleep and saw the women return, scooting under the van and under their own blankets. Only then did he sit up and stretch.

Fargo had to hand it to them. Their appearance, and their mannerisms were enough to fool anyone into believing they were men. They were even better than a male impersonator he had seen on stage in Denver, a professional actress who brought the house down with her portrayal of famous personages like George Washington and Davy Crockett.

Rising, Fargo rolled up his bedding. To restart the fire, he fed tinder to the few hot embers and blew lightly.

George Melton rolled over and yawned. "Have you made up your mind yet?" were the first words out of his mouth.

"I'll ride with you to Fort Laramie."

"Really?" Melton grinned. "What changed your mind? I could tell you weren't too keen on the notion."

"I wanted to get there sooner, but another couple of days shouldn't make too much of a difference," Fargo said. But the truth was, he hadn't come to a decision until he saw Carina step naked from the river.

A minute later the sisters came up behind him. Adopting a poker face so they wouldn't suspect he had learned their secret, Fargo said, "Care for some coffee, boys?"

"Don't call us that," Carina said. "We're grown men, and should be treated as such."

"You sure don't have the disposition of a man," Fargo said to get her goat, and was rewarded with a crimson tinge coloring her cheeks. "If I didn't know better, I'd swear you walked around with a broom handle shoved up your hind end."

Melton laughed loud enough to wake everyone else. "That's putting the whippersnapper in his place! Tarnation, boy, but you're pricklier than a cactus! Didn't that scrape at the Emporium teach you anything?"

Carina hadn't found Fargo's comment the least bit amusing. "It taught me there are two kinds of people in this world. Those who get stepped on, and those who stand up for themselves."

Melton sighed and said to Fargo, "The young always think they know it all, don't they?"

The crew bolted down cold elk and hot coffee for breakfast. After being given their share, the sisters moved over by their van and tore into their meat just as the men were doing, with a lot of chomping and grunting.

Now that Fargo knew their secret, he found their antics comical. It impressed him how they always contrived to screen their faces with their hats, or averted their gaze whenever anyone looked directly at them. Yet they did it so cleverly, making it all seem so natural, that no one else had caught on.

While Melton and the rest prepared the teams, Fargo saddled the Ovaro and rode back down the trail, past the bend. He had no trouble locating the tracks of their late-night visitor. The hoofprints were those of an extraordinarily large horse, and he recalled seeing a large bay tied to the hitch rail outside Honest Jack's. A large horse for a large man like Angus Stark.

The wagons were ready to roll when Fargo returned. He made it a point, as he rode past the last van, to wink at Carina and Carrie and say, "Try not to lag behind. The Sioux would love to get their hands on a pair of greenhorns like you."

Carina took exception and started to rise up out of the seat but Carrie yanked her down again. "Ignore him. He's just trying to bait you."

"And doing a fine job of it," Fargo bantered.

At the crack of Charlie's whip the small caravan lumbered forward. With dew-covered prairie on one side and the gently flowing river on the other, they wound along for mile after mile, maintaining a steady if plodding pace.

Chafing at their progress, Fargo almost regretted deciding to tag along. When the sun was directly overhead, Melton called a halt for half an hour so the horses could rest, and promptly pulled out the whiskey bottle.

Dismounting, Fargo stretched his legs by walking back and forth, then strolled to the river. Carrie and Carina were throwing flat stones, seeing how many times they could make them skip. When they saw him, they both tensed.

"What do you want?" Carina demanded.

"I came over to wash my hands," Fargo said innocently. Sinking onto a knee, he proceeded to do so. "The two of you could use a little washing up, too."

"How's that?" Carrie said.

"You go around with more dirt on your faces than ten-year-olds," Fargo said. "If you ask me, you both need baths."

Carina's jaw muscles twitched. "But we didn't ask you, did we?"

"Suit yourselves." Standing, Fargo dried his hands on his buckskins. "I just hope you change your minds before you get any riper."

"Riper?" Carrie repeated.

"Before you start smelling like a horse that's been in the hot sun too long. But then"—Fargo moved toward the wagons—"maybe you don't mind the odor. Melton did say you were fresh off the farm."

Out of the corner of an eye Fargo saw Carina grow as red as a beet. She would have lit into him if not for Carrie, who seized her wrist, then stared after him a good long while, her forehead knit.

The afternoon waned as slowly as the morning. To Fargo's mild surprise, they encountered no other travelers. Once they spooked several doe, and later a solitary buffalo appeared to the north, an old bull grazing by its lonesome.

Periodically Fargo came to where trees had been chopped down, dozens at a stroke. Based on how dry the stumps were, he calculated it had been done the week before. The trees were hauled out by wagon to be used as poles, Melton suggested, for the telegraph line. Apparently, Western Union planned to disperse crews from Fort Laramie, with some erecting poles and others stringing wire. They would push west until they met up with other crews who were driving eastward from Sacramento, California.

Evening came and went. Everyone turned in early except for Fargo, who stayed up past midnight to insure against unwanted visitors.

The next day was a repeat of the first.

On the third day, shortly after sunset, as they were gathered around the campfire waiting for the stew Charlie had thrown together to come to a boil, hooves hammered to the west.

Fargo motioned for the others to stay where they were, and snatching up the Henry, he moved into the shadows.

Before long, four riders drew rein just beyond the circle of firelight. They said and did nothing until Melton lifted an arm and called out, "Howdy, there. You're welcome to share our grub if you want."

The four men brought their mounts into the light. All four had the lean, pantherish stamp of hardcases. Two wore slickers. The third was a small, wiry Mexican wearing a sombrero. But it was the fourth man who piqued Fargo's interest the most. In his early thirties, he wore expensive store-bought clothes, all in black, and favored a gunbelt with a large silver buckle and silver studs. In the holster on his right hip rested an ivory-handled Smith and Wesson. He had a cruel slash for a mouth, and as he kneed his sorrel forward he smirked as if in ill-concealed contempt. "What have we here? More telegraph workers, I take it."

"You take it correctly, sir," Melton said, rising and introducing himself.

"They call me Dallas," the man drawled in a distinct twang that might indicate he was Texas born and bred, or could just as well be the Southern accent of someone from Kentucky.

"After the city by that name?" Melton asked.

Dallas didn't answer. Forking his left leg around his saddle horn, he regarded the workmen. "There must be fifty or sixty Western Union people at Fort Laramie already. Pretty soon there will be enough of you to start your own city."

The Mexican tittered. The other two riders might as well have been carved from wood.

Melton walked around the fire. "You've come from the fort, then?"

"Yesterday," Dallas said. "We've been riding hard ever since, and we're starved." He nodded at the pot. "I reckon we'll take you up on your offer."

"We have more than enough," Melton assured them.

"For us or for you, señor?" the small Mexican said, and tittered again.

Fargo stepped into the open, the Henry level at his waist. "For everyone. Unless you would rather go hungry."

The four riders reacted as if they had been pricked with pins. The Mexican's hand drifted toward his revolver, but stopped when Dallas uttered a curt laugh. "Well, what do you know, Valdez. A wolf among the sheep."

"A lot of wolves are abroad tonight," Fargo said.

"Do you have a handle, mister?" Dallas inquired.

"Yes," Fargo replied, but he didn't say what it was. He would rather keep them in the dark. They were potential trouble, even if Melton was too trusting to see it.

Chuckling, the old man slapped his leg. "Hell, don't be so modest. This here is Skye Fargo. Maybe you gents have heard of him?"

"No, señor," Valdez said.

"I have," Dallas declared, and scrutinized Fargo from head to toe. "You're the one who shot down Bob and Frank Jeffers."

"They were trying to buck me out in gore at the time," Fargo noted. Better known as the Texas Terrors, the Jeffers had been brutal outlaws who reaped a fate they richly deserved. "Were they friends of yours?"

"Never met the gentlemen," Dallas claimed.

Melton gestured. "Light and set a spell. We'd love the company. Maybe you can tell us the latest news."

At a nod from Dallas, the four men climbed down. Valdez walked to the pot, inhaled deeply, and smacked his lips. The pair in slickers hung back, roosting right where they were, sinking down cross-legged with their wrists on their knees.

"You'll have to forgive the Baxter boys," Dallas said, walking to the fire and holding his palms out to warm them. "They're not very sociable."

"No need to be shy around us," Melton said. "We're as friendly as can be. Isn't that right, fellas?"

The other members of the crew nodded.

Grinning like a cat about to eat the canary, Dallas pushed his hat back and hunkered over. "There can never be too much friendliness in this world of ours, can there?"

"Maybe someone should tell that to the Southerners who want to secede from the Union," Charlie thoughtlessly commented.

Dallas glanced up sharply. "And to all the Yankees who think they have the God-given right to dictate how the rest of the country should live."

Melton was taken aback by the man's vehemence. "You're for the South, I gather?"

"I'm for myself," Dallas said sullenly, then abruptly regained his composure. "As is anyone with a shred of common sense. Only a jackass would volunteer to die for a cause they don't have a stake in."

"Even if the cause is a noble one?" Carrie asked.

Fargo observed Valdez pivot and stare intently at her,

as if striving to see through the grime that caked her features.

Dallas laughed. "One man's nobility, sonny, is another man's stupidity. You can go off and fight a war for a bunch of pompous politicians if you want. But those politicians won't shed a tear if you take a bullet."

"A person should always do what's right," Carrie said, holding her ground.

Dallas laughed louder. "I bet you were the pride of your Sunday school class. But who's to say what's right and what isn't?"

Carrie answered, "Our conscience."

"Hell, cub," Dallas spat, "my conscience died from neglect about the time you were born."

"I feel sorry for you, then," Carrie said.

"Save your sympathy for those who want it," Dallas growled.

Fargo sat across from the quartet, the Henry in his lap. He didn't trust them as far as he could toss a wildcat, and he watched them closely, without being obvious, as they ate.

Dallas engaged George Melton in small talk about recent reports of Indian activity. The pair in slickers never uttered a word. Nor did Valdez, who was constantly peering out from under his sombrero at Carrie and Carina.

An hour after the newcomers arrived, Dallas gulped the last of his coffee and stood. "The night is still young, boys. Let's fan the wind."

"You're leaving?" Melton said. "Why not stay until morning? It's not safe to be on the go after dark."

"We'll take our chances," Dallas said. "We have to meet some friends of ours at a place on down the trail."

"Honest Jack's Trade and Liquor Emporium," Fargo said.

The four long riders swung toward him. "A lucky guess?" Dallas said.

"We ran into those friends of yours the other day," Fargo said. "Angus Stark, Brody, and Pawnee Tom."

Confusion etched the hardcases. "They told you about us?" Dallas said skeptically.

"They weren't able to tell us much of anything," Fargo said, and saw Melton and some of the other Western Union crew swap frightened glances, afraid he was about to reveal more than he should. "They were involved in a shootout."

"What?" Dallas took a step. "Who with? What was the outcome?"

"Two of your friends were shot," Fargo reported. "We didn't stick around afterward, so I can't say how many are still alive." Which was true as far as it went.

"What are we waitin' for?" one of the men in slickers asked Dallas impatiently.

"We should have been there to help them," said the other.

"Madre Dios!" Valdez exclaimed. "What if he was killed? What will we do without him? The whole thing was his idea, no?"

Dallas rounded on the *pistolero*. "Climb a tree and shout it out to the whole world, why don't you?" He pushed the Mexican toward their mounts. "Fork leather, leaky mouth. We're lighting a shuck for Jack's."

Without delay, without a word of thanks, the four men swiftly departed. Only after the pounding of their hoofbeats faded did anyone speak.

Letting out a long breath, Charlie said to Fargo, "For a second there I thought you were fixing to tell them it was you who shot Brody and that breed."

"What was that all about, anyway?" Melton asked. "How the dickens did you know they were bound for that two-faced trader's?"

Fargo had merely put two and two together. Honest Jack had mentioned that Stark and Brody had been hanging around his establishment for days. Why would they do that, unless they were waiting for someone? When Dallas mentioned meeting up with friends, it had all come together. "Be thankful they're gone," Fargo said.

"I know I am," Carrie commented.

Fargo imagined both women were. Valdez had displayed a disturbing amount of interest in them, almost as if the *pistolero* suspected the truth.

"I'll be thankful when we finally reach Fort Laramie and have the army to protect us," Melton said. "To be honest, this wilderness life isn't to my liking. I like to fall asleep at night knowing I'll live to see the next sunset."

"Who doesn't?" Fargo said, and helped himself to more stew.

4

Fort Laramie, like Fort Bridger and some others, had been a trading post before the army came along and bought it. Situated on the Laramie River approximately a mile above its junction with the North Platte, the post was first called Fort William, then Fort John. The army finally decided to name it after the river, and the name stuck.

Few people knew, as Skye Fargo did, that the river itself was named after a French trapper, one Jacques Laramie, slain by the Arapahos back in 1821.

The post was intended to protect the emigrants using the Oregon Trail by keeping a lid on the various hostile tribes in the region. It was considered one of the most important on the frontier, and the officers assigned there were some of the most experienced the U.S. Army boasted.

Each day the fort bustled with activity from dawn until dusk. Emigrants by the wagon load, scores of frontiersmen in dusty buckskins, and friendly Indians mingled in a boisterous welter of humanity. Fortunately, the troopers were on hand to insure that no one got out of line. Those who did were promptly escorted from the premises.

Fargo had visited Fort Laramie more times than he could recall, but he had never seen it so crowded. Dallas had not been exaggerating about the number of Western Union people. If anything, he had underestimated the total by quite a bit. Western Union wagons and vans were lined up to one side of the parade ground in long rows, ready to head out as soon as the order was given.

Melton bid Fargo good-bye just inside the gate. "Thanks for sticking with us," the oldster said. "If we can ever repay the favor, you only have to ask."

Fargo nodded. The crew rolled their wagons toward the parade ground, and as the last van clattered by, Fargo grinned at the girls and got in his parting shot. "Take care, you two."

"Will do, Mr. Fargo," Carrie politely responded.

"If you ever get tired of wearing those baggy duds and put on some dresses, look me up. I'll treat you to a night you'll never forget."

Chuckling at their astonishment, Fargo reined the pinto toward the headquarters building, where he assumed he would find the man he was to meet. He had to thread through a sea of people. Shoshones, wearing their finest blankets and beaded garments; grizzled mountain men in from the high country; pilgrims bound for the promised lands of Oregon or California. And other, less savory characters, cut from the same coarse cloth as Angus Stark and the four long riders, men who lived by their wits and their weapons, more often than not on the shady side of the law.

The hitch rail was practically full. Fargo had to shoulder a mare aside to make room for the Ovaro. Yanking the Henry from the saddle scabbard, he cradled it in his arm and moved toward the building, only to be grabbed from behind and spun around.

"Fargo! You came!"

"Why wouldn't I?"

Major Edward Canby was a career military man, a professional soldier whose ramrod bearing and neatly pressed uniform were in keeping with his spit-and-polish outlook. He warmly pumped Fargo's hand. "I was beginning to worry you wouldn't."

"You saved my life once," Fargo said. "I owe you, remember?" He genuinely liked the man. Unlike a lot

40

of officers, Canby wasn't a conceited stuffed shirt. "Where was it I saw you last? Fort Bridger?"

"That it was." Canby looked both ways, then drew Fargo away from those nearest to them. "I can't thank you enough for coming. I'm in a bind and I need your help." He paused. "Or, rather, the U.S. Army is in a bind, and we've nowhere else to turn."

"I'm listening."

"Let's go to my office," Canby suggested, pointing at the adjutant's building to the north. "I'll send an orderly for coffee and a bite to eat."

"Sounds good to me," Fargo said. "Lead the way." It was almost noon and he was ready for some food.

"Can you believe this?" the major said over a shoulder as they waded through the throng. "It's a madhouse! Over a hundred telegraph workers are here to work on the next stretch of wire, and more are due in next week."

"Creating problems, are they?"

"My friend, you don't know the half of it. General Oliver directed us to provide them with shelter and sustenance, but he never told us how many would show up. They've taxed our stores to the limit. We've had to requisition more supplies from Fort Leavenworth just to feed them."

"So you'll be glad to see them go," Fargo guessed.

"I'll get drunk and dance a jig," Major Canby said. "But they're not our main concern at the moment."

"Are the Sioux acting up again?"

"We've had a few reports of a small war party harassing travelers. No scalps have been taken, though. That might change once all the telegraph workers fan out across the prairie. They'll be tempting targets for every hostile this side of the Rockies."

Canby's office was Spartan. As he sank into a chair behind his desk, Fargo did the same across from him. The major hustled an orderly off, and within five minutes they had a pot of coffee and a plate of buttered rolls.

Removing his hat, Canby idly stroked his waxed mustache. "I won't keep you in suspense any longer. Have you heard of a man called Tuck Garson?"

"Who hasn't?" Fargo said. Wherever he went, that name cropped up like a bad odor that wouldn't go away. "Is he why you sent for me?"

Major Canby nodded. "Ordinarily, we don't involve ourselves in civilian matters. But the Interior Department has expanded our scope. From now on we're to protect the emigrants from outlaws as well as renegade Indians, and Garson is at the top of our list."

"Are the stories they tell about him true?"

"He's vile beyond belief. A murderous butcher. About ten days ago his gang massacred a family bound for Oregon. They were with a wagon train, but they dropped behind when one of their wheels came loose. The wagon master rode back to check on them when they didn't catch up, and found their bodies. The husband, the wife, two sons, and a little girl, all slashed to ribbons." Canby shuddered. "I'm not squeamish, as you well know. But when I saw them . . ." He broke off.

Fargo remembered that Canby had seen service in the Southwest and had witnessed brutal Apache depredations firsthand. For him to be so affected by Garson's handiwork spoke volumes. "It was that bad?"

"What they did to that poor woman and her daughter . . ." Again the major stopped, racked by intense emotion. Taking deep breaths, he calmed himself. "Sorry. I have a wife and daughter of my own. It struck a chord."

"What is it, exactly, you want of me?"

"We want Tuck Garson dead."

Fargo bit into the roll. He wholeheartedly agreed the cutthroat had to be stopped, but the officer was overlooking something. "I'm not an assassin for hire," he quietly noted.

"I know, I know," Canby said quickly. "And I'm not asking you to kill him for us. All I want, all the army needs, is for you to *find* him. Once you have, get word to me and we'll take care of the rest."

"Your own scouts have tried," Fargo said. It was a statement, not a question.

"Tried and tried again. But Garson always manages to give them the slip. It doesn't help matters any that we don't know what the man looks like. Every one of his victims has died before they could describe him." The major was a study in frustration. "Nor does it help that he uses an alias. Word is, he goes by another name most of the time. He could be anyone, anywhere. He could be here at the post, right this minute, walking among us and laughing at our incompetence."

"His gang must know."

"But locating them is as difficult as locating Garson. Hell, we don't even know how many there are. We've had conflicting reports. As high as fifteen, as low as eight."

"No names?"

"I wish. The whole gang could be standing right outside my window with Garson, and I wouldn't know it."

"So you have no information at all," Fargo summed it up. "How do you expect me to find them?"

"Sooner or later Garson will strike again. When he does, you can track him to his lair. That's all you have to do. Don't confront him. Get word to me. I'll have an entire detachment ready to ride out at a moment's notice."

"And in the meantime I stay at the fort, twiddling my thumbs?" Fargo wasn't keen on the notion, but it was a small sacrifice to make when weighed in the balance against the lives he could save.

"I'll be honest with you," Canby said. "It could be days. It could be weeks. Tuck Garson seems to pick his prey at random. There's no rhyme or reason to his attacks that I can discern. Unless . . ." The major paused.

"Unless what?"

"He's from Kentucky, so the story goes. Which means his sympathies might lie with the South in the coming clash. General Oliver is worried there might be more to Garson's raids than we suspect. That maybe he's been sent to stir things up, to sow widespread carnage and divert troops from the East where they are most needed."

"Garson will do all that with just fifteen men?" Fargo said.

"I know. When the general first mentioned it to me it sounded as ridiculous as it must sound now. But we can't discount the possibility. It's added incentive, as if any were needed, for us to put an end to Garson's rampages." Canby spread his hands on the desk. "Will you do it? Will you help us?"

Fargo bit into the roll again, chewed thoughtfully, then swallowed. "I'll help. But on my terms."

"Name them."

"I won't be rushed, I won't be bossed around. I do things my way. When Garson strikes again, I go out alone. A bunch of troopers would only slow me down."

"Done and done." Canby smiled broadly. "For the first time in months, I think we have a chance to end his bloodthirsty spree."

A quarter of an hour later Fargo stepped out into the bright afternoon sun. He had agreed to meet the major later for supper. Until then his time was his own, and his first order of business was to stable the pinto. Squinting in the harsh glare, he ambled toward the hitch rail.

The sutler's, Fargo saw, was doing brisk business. Indians had brought in pelts to swap for blankets and trinkets. Mountain men were stocking up on ammunition and essentials. Emigrants were buying everything under the sun.

On a whim Fargo changed direction; he was low on cartridges for the Henry. But getting inside took some doing. Customers were jammed together like ants in an anthill, a dozen bellowing for assistance at a time. A handful of clerks scampered about like grasshoppers, vainly seeking to meet the demand for their services.

Fargo shouldered his way to the counter and tried to get a clerk's attention.

"Wait your turn, young man," an elderly woman on his left said sternly. "I was here before you were."

"Yes, ma'am," Fargo said, grinning, while giving a courtly bow. "I wouldn't dream of being rude to a lovely lady like yourself."

"Oh, pshaw," the woman gushed, as pleased as could be.

Behind him someone snapped, "And you would know all about how to treat ladies, wouldn't you, mister?"

Fargo turned. Carrie and Carina looked fit to tear into him tooth and nail. "Fellas," he said, nodding. "Are you here for chewing tobacco? Or to buy some new long underwear for the winter?"

"We need to see you," Carrie said.

"About dresses and such," Carina added.

"How about if I meet you outside in a couple of minutes?" Fargo proposed.

"No longer than that, though," Carrie said, poking him with her forefinger. "You hear me, big man?"

Scowling, both sisters stalked off.

The elderly matron next to Fargo clucked like a biddy hen. "Pushy cusses, aren't they? What's come over the young folks today? They have no manners whatsoever."

"Spare the rod and spoil the child," Fargo said.

"Ain't that the truth," the woman agreed. "Why, when I was little, if I gave my parents any sass, Pa hauled me out to the woodshed and took a switch to my backside. Best thing he ever did. It taught me that doing wrong was wrong. If more younguns nowadays were tanned until they screamed, there would be a lot less rudeness in this world."

A clerk arrived just as the matron launched into an account of each and every time she had been switched.

Shortly thereafter, with a new box of .44-caliber ammunition in hand, Fargo stepped from the store and immediately acquired a pair of shadows, one on either side.

"What have you guys been up to?" he asked, and couldn't suppress a laugh.

"We need to talk," Carrie reiterated.

"In private," Carina said.

Fargo scanned the swirling sea of buckskin, homespun and uniforms. "Where do you suggest? The top of the flagpole?"

"Funny man," Carina said, gripping his elbow. "Our van is nice and quiet. We're not likely to be disturbed there."

"Not when Mr. Melton and the rest of the crew are busy drowning in rotgut," Carrie declared, taking his other arm.

Fargo let them steer him through the crowd to the west end of the parade ground. Their van was parked in the last row near the palisade, as isolated a spot as they were likely to find anywhere on the post. Carrie looked both ways, then opened the narrow door at the rear and gestured for him to go in.

"Ladies first," Fargo said.

Carina, ever the hothead, gave him a shove. Or tried to. The best she could do was make him sway slightly. "If I were a real man, I'd wallop the stuffing out of you!"

"If you were a real man, you wouldn't have any reason to be mad at me," Fargo observed, and climbed on up. Bundles of telegraph wire were stacked to the left. On the right hung various tools. He moved forward and roosted on one of the stacks. "Now suppose you tell me what this is all about."

Neither of the sisters replied right away. Carrie had shut the door, plunging them in gloom. There were no windows, only a slit for ventilation at the front.

Carina lit a small candle and placed it on a tiny shelf. "Now let's get to it," she said brusquely. "How did you catch on to us? What gave us away?"

"Your body," Fargo said. "I saw you bathing in the river."

"You did?"

"I warned you!" Carrie said, angrily smacking her sister's arm. "Time and again I said it was too risky to take baths, but you wouldn't listen! You had to do things your way! And now our secret is out!"

Carina hadn't taken her eyes off Fargo. "Did you like what you saw?"

"Carina!" Carrie shoved the darker-haired girl, nearly spilling her onto the wire. "You're absolutely shameless, do you know that?"

"I like what I saw a lot," Fargo said, his gaze roving over Carina's baggy clothes. "A man would never guess to look at you now that you're a beautiful woman."

"Beautiful?" Carina said. Coyly clasping her hands behind her back, she swayed her hips enticingly. "Do you really think so?"

"Carina!" Carrie squealed again. "This isn't the time or the place." She faced Fargo. "Look, we need to know what you plan to do. Are you going to report us to Western Union? Or to the army?"

"Why would I do that?" Fargo asked.

"Because we're women. Because we've taken jobs under false pretenses." In her stress, Carrie was speaking in her normal, higher-pitched voice. "Hear us out. That's all I ask. And if you still want to turn us in afterward, that's up to you."

"There's a reason we're masquerading as men," Carina said.

Fargo shifted, making himself comfortable. "This should be interesting. I'm all ears, ladies."

Carina giggled. "Oh, I think there's a lot more to you than a pair of ears, big man. You're about the handsomest jasper I've laid eyes on in a coon's age."

"You should work in a brothel, Sis," Carrie griped. "Do me a favor, will you? Stand there and keep quiet until I'm done or you'll have him thinking we're both sluts." Rolling her eyes, she asked Fargo, "Do you really want to hear our story?"

"I wouldn't miss it for the world." Fargo was serious.

They had him enormously curious. And Carina's sugges-
tive looks had stirred him lower down.

"We're from Ohio," Carrie began. "You know that
much from Mr. Melton. You also know we lived on a
farm. But the farm was on its last legs. We'd lost our
crops to drought, and the few cows we had were skin
and bones. Then, about six months ago, we lost our father. He was digging a new well and slipped. The fall
broke his neck."

"I'm sorry," Fargo said.

Carrie's eyes misted over at the memory. Blinking
back the tears, she resumed. "It had been just the three
of us for the longest while. Our ma died when Carina
and I were little." She dabbed an eye. "Without Pa, we
knew there was no hope of making the farm pay off.
We were desperate for money."

"Why didn't you sell the farm?" Fargo wondered. "It
had to be worth something."

"It wasn't ours to sell. Pa didn't leave a will. Even if
he had, he owed so much to the bank, we wouldn't have
seen a penny." Carrie's voice had grown thick with emotion, and she coughed. "So we looked around for jobs.
There wasn't much work to be had, though. Not decent
work. Not work that paid well."

Carina broke her silence. "Oh, there were seamstress
positions galore, but we've never been much good at
sewing. We've worked outdoors all the time, tending the
animals and planting crops and whatnot."

"A gentleman in Columbus wanted to hire us as print-
er's apprentices," Carrie said. "But he was only willing
to pay us a pittance." She made a sound reminiscent of
a she-cat about to strike. "That was the problem with
all the jobs we applied for."

"Women are never paid as much as men," Carina said
resentfully. "Even when a woman does the same kind
of work a man does, the woman is paid half as much."

"Or less," Carrie amended.

"A lot less," Carina said.

Fargo had heard the same lament before. Women

were tired of being treated as inferior, of always being shortchanged in the workplace. When he was in St. Louis a couple of years ago, the city had been abuzz over a woman named Susan B. Anthony, who was going around the country urging women everywhere to rise up against their "Saxon male oppressors."

"Then we saw an advertisement in the newspaper," Carrie had gone on. "Western Union was hiring linemen. No experience necessary."

"And the positions paid three times as much as we could make anywhere else," Carina said. "There was only one hitch."

"The jobs were for men," Fargo interjected.

Both sisters nodded. "But we didn't let that stop us," Carrie said. "We remembered seeing a lady on stage once who dressed up like a man so well, no one could tell the difference. We decided to try the same thing."

"We practiced at it," Carina revealed. "We tried on different clothes until we found what looked best. For hours on end we walked like men and talked like men until we could do it well enough that no one would suspect."

Carrie laughed lightly. "We were astonished when it worked. You could have knocked us over with feathers."

"We walked into the Western Union office, answered a few questions, and were hired on the spot," Carina said. "It's been rough at times but we've hoodwinked everyone since."

"Until you came along," Carrie said.

"One word from you to the telegraph company and we're out of work," Carina stated. "They wouldn't care how good a job we've done."

"They'd probably demand all our back pay, and take us to court if we didn't make good," Carrie predicted.

Mute appeal and fear were mirrored in their expressions. They had bared their souls and were in dire dread of Fargo spoiling everything. "Ladies," he assured them, "your secret is safe with me."

"Do you really mean that?" Carrie asked.

"I'm not in the habit of lying."

"Why are you being so considerate?" Carina asked. "Most males would leap at the chance to expose us and put two females in their proper place."

"You have a lower opinion of us than we deserve," Fargo responded.

"You could have fooled us," Carrie said bitterly. "Most men don't want their womenfolk to ever step foot out of the kitchen. Unless it's to lie in bed, pushing out one baby after another."

Fargo leaned back, his fingers intertwined behind his head. "I like the bed idea, but it would be too crowded with all those little ones."

Carina tittered and started toward him but was stopped by Carrie. "Don't you dare! I know what you're thinking, and it's too dangerous."

"How so?" Carina said. "He already knows all there is to know about us."

"Except your real last name," Fargo mentioned. "Which I take it isn't Carrington."

"It's Darrwood," Carina said. "Carrie and Carina Darrwood."

"Ah." Fargo chuckled. "Darr and Wood. Simple but clever." He winked at Carina. "Now what was it you wanted to say?"

Brushing past Carrie, Carina sashayed up to the Trailsman.

With her baggy clothes, floppy hat and grimy face she was about as appealing as a bump on a log, a situation Fargo remedied by envisioning the twin mounds under her shirt, and how her bosom had glistened with watery drops when she waded out of the river.

"I'm grateful to you for not giving us away," Carina said.

Fargo knowingly took the bait. "How grateful?"

Before Carina could reply, Carrie flung the door wide and stormed out. "Look me up when you're done playing the tart," she said, and slammed it.

"Don't mind her," Carina said. "She's just jealous."

"Could have fooled me," Fargo mimicked her. "Your sister looked mad enough to bean me with a rock."

Carina inched nearer, so near their legs brushed. "I shouldn't tell you this, but I took a hankering to you the moment I set eyes on you."

"Did you, now," Fargo said, placing his hands on her hips. Her body was warm and yielding, and at his touch a ripple coursed through her entire body.

"You are so naughty," Carina said impishly, bending so her mouth was now a finger's width from his.

"You haven't seen anything yet."

"Show me."

5

Skye Fargo slowly molded his mouth to Carina Darrwood's. Her soft lips parted and her silken tongue darted out to entwine in a velvet dance with his. A low groan escaped her as Carina pressed against him, her hands looping around his broad shoulders. She clung to him as if afraid he would get up and leave.

When, at passionate length, their kiss ended, Carina closed her eyes and grinned. "Mmm. That was nice."

"I'm just getting started," Fargo teased.

Carina opened her eyes again. Raw passion blazed like twin cauldrons in both. "It's been so long since a man has touched me. So damn long! I couldn't so much as give one a second look for fear of giving our secret away."

"It must be hard on you," Fargo sympathized. And he meant it. He could no more go without women than he could without air to breathe, so for a woman like her to have to go without men must have been torture.

"You don't know the half of it," Carina said sorrowfully. "The sacrifices I make! All so my sister and I can make as much money as men do."

"How long do you intend to keep this up?" Fargo asked.

"Our plan is to work our way to California," Carina revealed. "We've heard tell it's awful pretty, and the folks there are supposed to be as friendly as can be."

"Will you keep on working for the telegraph company?"

"We haven't thought that far ahead," Carina said,

then laced her warm fingers behind his neck. "And you talk too much, you know that?"

Again she locked her lips to Fargo's in a fiery kiss that hinted at the true depths of her carnal craving. Her mouth was lush and ripe, sweet fruit for the offering, and Fargo sucked on her delicious tongue as if it were candy. Carina squirmed and cooed like a dove, her fingers rising to run through his hair. His hat fell beside them.

"Oh, my," she husked as they parted. "You sure are a natural, aren't you? You about take a girl's breath away."

Fargo took off her floppy hat and dropped it next to his. When he ran a hand through her short hair as she had just done to his, she frowned. "Something wrong?" he asked.

"I used to have such gorgeous hair. Clear down to here." Carina touched her waist. "I hated having to cut it but Carrie insisted. She was worried that all it would take was a gust of wind to expose us."

"You're lovely as you are," Fargo said.

Carina laughed. "You, sir, are a terrible liar. With these clothes and the dirt on my face, I'm as frumpy as can be."

"Well, I don't have a washcloth handy," Fargo said, "but the clothes are easy to take care of." So saying, he tugged on her baggy shirt, pulling it up out of her pants. She grinned seductively, the pink tip of her tongue jutting between her lips, as Fargo slowly slid his right hand underneath her shirt and placed his palm flat against her smooth stomach. He felt her quiver in anticipation.

"Between you, me, and the hitch rail, I'm glad you found us out," Carina said huskily. "I've needed a man so bad, I can't hardly sleep at night."

"Then let's not keep you waiting any longer," Fargo said, swooping his hand to her right breast. Covering it, he squeezed hard enough to elicit a gasp.

"Ohhhhh. Yessssss."

Using three fingers, Fargo tweaked her nipple. Carina

bit her lower lip and moaned in delight. Almost frantic with lust, she unbuttoned her shirt to permit him access to her inner charms. Fargo immediately placed his mouth on her left mound and sucked, his tongue swirling the nipple around and around while his hand continued to massage her other breast.

Carina tilted her head back and wheezed like a bellows. Her fingers gripped his hair, her hips grinding against him. "More. I want more."

Fargo lowered a hand and undid her thin leather belt. Her pants were so loose, the moment the belt was undone they plopped down around her ankles. She had on a woman's frilly undergarment, which he slid down to her feet, baring the downy thatch that had tantalized him the other day at the river.

Switching his mouth to her other tender globe, Fargo dropped both hands to her hips and ran his fingers over her firm bottom. Her legs were gloriously smooth, her skin satiny. He brought a hand around to her knee and roved upward along exquisite inner thighs.

Carina bowed her head and leaned against him, her eyelids hooded. "You have me on pins and needles, handsome," she said softly.

Fargo stopped just below the junction of her legs, drawing out the suspense. He kissed her throat, kissed between her breasts, kissed her stomach. His nostrils tingled at the heady fragrance she gave off, a living bouquet trembling with pent-up desire.

A slight noise outside gave Fargo momentary pause. He listened but it wasn't repeated.

"What are you waiting for, damn you?" Carina complained.

Sliding his right hand higher, Fargo cupped her nether mound. It was so sudden, she rose up onto her toes as if seeking to take wing. He ran a finger across her moist slit, exciting her further. Her nether lips parted, his finger brushing her swollen knob.

Involuntarily, Carina started to cry out, but she stifled it by clenching her teeth.

Fargo flicked his finger a few times, then ever so slowly inserted the end of it into her hot tunnel. Her slick molten walls rippled and contracted. His finger was hardly all the way in when Carina began thrusting against his hand in abandon, humping her womanhood against him in a seeming effort to impale herself.

Fargo stroked her several more times. That was all it took. With a violent start, Carina Darrwood exploded, her luscious body convulsing in a paroxysm of release as she clamped his head to her bosom.

"Oh! Oh! Ahhhh! I'm coming already! I'm coming!"

That she did, gushing like a fountain, a harbinger of pleasures to come. Fargo plunged his finger up and in, over and over, until Carina mewed like a kitten and folded on top of him, spent in more ways than one. He eased her onto his lap, and her cheek sagged onto his shoulder.

"Sorry," Carina panted.

"You have nothing to apologize for," Fargo said. He kissed her neck, then fastened his mouth on her earlobe. She wriggled and sighed, her left hand straying to the iron bulge in his pants.

"What have we here?" Carina said with a smirk. Her fingers pried first at his gun belt, then his buckskins.

The contact of her warm palm on his manhood provoked waves of delight. Leaning back, Fargo let her do as she pleased. She began to lightly rub his shaft. A constriction formed in his throat and he had to cough to clear it. Her mouth sought his neck as she cupped him lower down.

Adrift in a sea of sensation, Fargo barely noticed when she bent down. Her palm was replaced by wetness, and now his own hips were moving of their own accord. It took every ounce of concentration he possessed to maintain his self-control.

After a while, Carina straightened, her face flushed, her mouth parted in a delectable oval. Propping her hands on his shoulders, she straddled him and raised herself up. Then, reaching between them, she gripped his redwood and held it steady while she fed it up into her velvet sheath.

They were joined, two bodies made one. Fargo could feel her womanhood enfold him, could feel how wonderfully wet and tight she was. For a minute they both just sat there, reveling in the rapture.

Carina moved first, rocking her hips. In response, Fargo started a thrusting motion, matching his rhythm to the tempo of her movements. Their mouths glued together, and Fargo's hands rose to her pert, heaving apples. When he pinched both hard nipples, Carina moaned long and loud.

She was being too loud, Fargo thought. He didn't say anything, though. Overcome by sensual bliss, he reared up into her, pumping upward over and over, lifting them both off their makeshift seat.

Fargo couldn't say what made him glance toward the door. Maybe it was the sixth sense he had honed living in the wilds. Maybe it was a gust of air, or a faint sound he unconsciously registered. Whatever the case, he looked toward it and glimpsed a shadowed shape pull back from sight. The door was swung almost shut.

Someone had been spying on them. Fargo wanted to go see who it was, but at that exact moment Carina crested, spurting anew in an orgasm to end all orgasms. Wrapping her limbs around him, she ground her bottom in wild delirium. There was no checking the tide, no stopping her.

"Yes, Skye! Yessssss!"

Fargo had no choice but to let the lurker go. One eye on the door, he matched Carina's ardor, lancing up into her with heightened speed and vigor. His pole pulsed, on the verge of release. Another few seconds and there was no holding back. Pinpoints of light flared before his eyes and the inside of the van spun like a whirlwind.

Gradually, Fargo coasted to a stop. Covered with perspiration, he heard his heart pounding and the flutter of his own breath. Time drifted at a snail's pace. They leaned against one another, Carina nuzzling his neck.

"I can't thank you enough."

Fargo kissed her forehead. "We should get dressed."

"What's your hurry?" Grinning, Carina wriggled her fanny. "Once is nice but twice is heaven."

"Someone was watching us," Fargo said, prying her hands off his shoulders.

"Someone was *what*?" Carina jumped up off of him as if she had burned her backside. On seeing the partially open door, she unleashed a string of unladylike oaths while swiftly dressing.

Fargo hitched his pants up and buckled his belt. "Could it have been your sister?" Some women liked to watch others make love, although he wouldn't have pegged Carrie as the kind. She was too straitlaced, too prim and proper.

"If it was, I'll strangle her," Carina vowed. Wedging her floppy hat on her head, she stormed past him.

"Wait for me," Fargo said, but hotheaded as Carina was, she did no such thing. He donned his hat and hastened out.

Carina was halfway down the row of wagons, stomping like a mad heifer.

"Wait!" Fargo called, but he might as well have saved his breath. Closing the door, he turned to follow. Suddenly, over by the palisade, footsteps pattered. He sprang past the van and spotted someone fleeing along the base of the wall, a skinny man in homespun clothes. He immediately gave chase.

The man flew to the south until he was near a building. Darting toward it, he turned his head to hide his features and sprinted around the corner.

Fargo reached the building less than ten seconds later, but by then the Peeping Tom had blended into the crush of people milling about the parade ground. Fargo barreled into them but saw no one remotely resembling his quarry.

Smacking a fist into his palm in annoyance, Fargo headed toward the wagons to find Carina. Instead, he spied Carrie, seated all alone on a bench near the quartermaster's. She looked up in surprise when he plunked down beside her.

"The two of you done already? My sister must be ill. Usually she doesn't let go of a man until she'd drained him dry."

"We were interrupted," Fargo said. "Someone was spying on us. I was hoping it was you."

"Me?" Carrie's green eyes flashed. "I have better things to do than watch my sister indulge her lust. I—" Carrie stopped as the full import hit her. "Wait a minute! Someone saw the two of you? Then they know Carina is a woman! We're ruined."

"Maybe not," Fargo said, but she didn't hear him.

"We'll be fired! All the trouble we've gone to, all the hardships we've endured, and it counts for nothing because my stupid sister can't keep a rein on her amorous nature! I warned her, but she wouldn't listen! She never does!"

"Are you done throwing a fit?" Fargo said when Carrie paused long enough for him to get a word in edgewise.

"I haven't even begun!" She began to rise. "When I get my hands on that pigheaded brat, I'll—"

"Simmer down," Fargo said, grabbing her wrist. "It might not be as bad as you think."

"How do you figure?"

"Maybe it was someone passing by. Someone who doesn't know either of you from Eve. Your secret might still be safe."

"If only we were that lucky!" Carrie frowned and gripped the edge of the bench. "But I've learned to always expect the worst. Life has a habit of kicking us in the teeth just when things are going our way."

Out of the throng stalked Carina. Marching up, she reached out to grab Carrie by the shirt, then blinked and glanced at Fargo. "Oh, God. I can tell by the look on her face it wasn't her, was it?"

"Why don't you ask me?" Carrie said curtly.

"No, it wasn't her," Fargo confirmed, scanning the

post for sign of anyone who might be unduly interested in them. But there was no one, and he was about to turn to the sisters when George Melton appeared, striding purposely toward them with an air of great urgency.

Fargo poked Carrie. "Then again, maybe it was someone who knows you." He nodded at the white-haired crew boss.

The women blanched, Carrie recoiling as if she had been slapped. Too flabbergasted to say anything, they stared at the old-timer as if he were the Reaper come to claim them.

"Here you boys are!" Melton said. "I've been searching all over." He gazed from one to the other. "Say, what's the matter? Both of you look sickly. Are you coming down with something?"

Carrie started to answer in her natural voice, caught herself, and, coughing, lowered it. "We're a little peaked, I reckon. And I might have a cold coming on."

"Well, you'd better get a good night's sleep. We head out in the morning."

"So soon?" Carina said.

"I just had a meeting with Mr. Williams, the supervisor. All Western Union wagons are to leave at dawn under military escort. We're to head south until we get to where the wire is being strung, then each crew will go to its assigned area." Melton patted a pocket. "He gave me a map that shows the section we're to do."

"Is this all you wanted?" Carrie asked.

"Isn't it enough?" Melton rejoined. "I was hoping we'd get to rest up at the fort a few days. But the company is bound and determined to complete the job ahead of schedule, even if they work us to death."

The sisters were smiling now that their worst fear hadn't come to pass. "My pa used to say that a little work never hurt anyone," Carina commented.

"We're looking forward to getting out there and getting it done," Carrie added.

Melton made a sound reminiscent of a goose being throttled. "Anyone ever mention that you boys are a mite weird? No one in their right mind *likes* to work. The object in life is to get out of doing as much work as you can so you have more time for what really counts. Namely, drinking."

"All that liquor will kill you one of these days," Carrie predicted.

"We all die eventually, sonny," Melton said. "Besides, I've lived longer than most already. I might as well spend my remaining years doing what I like best." Chortling, he walked off. "Be seeing you. I've got to find some of the others yet."

Carrie waited until he was well gone, then said, "Thank goodness! Our secret is still safe! No thanks to you, Sis!"

"Don't start in on me again," Carina warned. "I'm not a nun. I can't go without, like you seem able to do." She plucked at Carrie's sleeve. "Now why don't we bury the hatchet and go shopping? There are a few things we need to buy before we head out tomorrow."

"You go on. I'll catch up in a minute. I want to finish talking to Skye."

"About what?" Carina asked suspiciously.

"Nothing that concerns you," Carrie said, giving her sibling a push. "Just go, will you? I'll only be a minute."

Carina hesitated.

"I give you my word it's not about you," Carrie insisted. "Please. For once will you do what I ask without giving me grief?"

"One minute is all you get," Carina said, threading into the crowd.

Carrie shifted toward Fargo and snapped, "All right. Out with it. What are your intentions concerning my sister?"

"I thought you said it wasn't about her."

"I lied," Carrie confessed. "She's younger than me, and I have to look out for her whether she likes it or not. So I want to know what your intentions are, specifically whether you intend to ask for her hand in wedlock?"

"No," Fargo said. He wasn't one of those who lied to

60

women to curry their favor. "I never made any such promise."

"Good."

Fargo wasn't sure he had heard correctly. Most women were more interested in a long-term commitment than they let on, even when they claimed otherwise. "Good?"

"Carina isn't the type to tie herself down to one fellow. She goes through men like most women go through clothes. Or she did, until we landed these jobs and she had to change her ways."

Fargo had a thought. "Whose idea was it?"

"To disguise ourselves as men?" Carrie smiled slyly. "It was my brainstorm. It takes money to start a new life and this is the only way we can save it up." She rose. "We were desperate at the time. Practically broke. If the telegraph work hadn't come along when it did, there's no telling how low we would have sunk. Carina was ready to sell her body, if need be, but I would never let it come to that. I'd rob banks first."

Fargo watched the older sister blend into the mix of emigrants and frontiersmen. Stretching, he went to stand, then froze. A face had appeared in the throng, a sinister face he had seen once before, a face that had no business being there. It was Valdez!

Surging up off the bench, Fargo moved to head the Mexican off. He had to stop for a column of soldiers filing by, and when he moved on, he couldn't spot him. The telltale sombrero had vanished amid a bevy of people flocking toward the sutler's.

Fargo was puzzled. The small hardcase had been on his way to Honest Jack's Emporium with Dallas and the Baxter brothers. What was he doing at Fort Laramie? There hadn't been time for the four of them to reach Honest Jack's and then hightail it back. Either they had lied, or they had changed their minds and come to the post instead.

Rotating a full 360 degrees on the heel of a boot, Fargo looked and looked. Just when he was convinced it was hopeless, he spotted the sombrero weaving toward the main gate.

Fargo followed, thinking the others must be at the fort, too, and that it would be wise for Major Canby to question them to find out if they were, in fact, part of Tuck Garson's gang.

Valdez bore toward a hitch rail just inside the sally port and swung astride a dun. Reining around, he was out the gate before Fargo could get close enough to stop him. Once outside, the *pistolero* reined to the left.

Fargo ran to the east stockade, which was a lot closer than the gate or his own horse, and quickly scaled a ladder leaning against the parapet. Stepping to the wall, he surveyed the rutted trail for as far as the eye could see.

A quarter of a mile out, snaking toward the fort, was a wagon train. Along the tree-lined river scores of vehicles were parked, covered wagons in all sizes. A pair of troopers were just exiting the main gate. But there wasn't any sign of the Mexican.

Fargo's puzzlement grew. Valdez should still be in sight. The only possible explanation was that the gunman had turned into the trees somewhere.

"Excuse me, sir. Civilians aren't allowed up here."

A young trooper had stepped from the guard tower. Rather than argue, Fargo hastened down and cut across the parade ground toward the Ovaro. He had an excellent chance of finding Valdez if he acted right away. But the press of people hindered him, and try as he might, when he finally reached his stallion, the gunman had enough of a lead to be halfway to Missouri. Still, Fargo hiked his foot to step into the stirrups.

"Mr. Fargo, sir?" Another young trooper had stepped around from in front of the pinto. He wore a typical shell jacket and an infantry forage cap, or a kepi, as they were called.

"What is it?" Fargo impatiently asked.

"Major Canby's compliments, sir," the trooper formally declared. "He requests your presence right away."

"Can't it wait?"

"I'm afraid not, sir. He was most insistent." The trooper motioned toward the building housing Canby's office. "Please, sir."

Reluctantly, Fargo did as he was bid. "Have you any idea what it's about?"

"The major didn't see fit to say, sir. But I gather something important has happened. All the officers are to report to the commander within the hour, and there's a talk of mustering most of the troops to ride out soon."

Fargo couldn't see that happening, not with so many emigrants camped nearby who needed protecting. "It sounds as if you're going to war," he remarked.

"I hope so, sir," the young man said. "I didn't enlist to spend every waking hour scrubbing floors and sweeping out stables. I joined up to fight." He saluted a lieutenant passing by and the officer returned it. "We've drilled and drilled until I can perform maneuvers in my sleep. Now I want a chance to show what I've learned. To prove I'm half the soldier I think I am."

Fargo looked at him. "Have you ever shot anyone, Private?"

"Private Harrison, sir. Not yet, no. But what does that have to do with anything?"

"Taking another person's life should never be taken lightly," Fargo said. When it was, those who did ended up like Angus Stark or Dallas.

"It's what they train me to do, though, isn't it, sir? To kill? That's what being a professional soldier is all about."

"Killing is only part of it," Fargo said. "It's more important to know when to kill, and when not to."

"That's for the officers to decide, sir," Private Harrison said. "All I do is follow orders. But one day that will change. I'll rise through the ranks and become a captain. Or maybe even a colonel."

"I hope you live that long, Private."

Soldiers were streaming in and out of the adjutant's building. The hallway was filled with knots of enlisted personnel and noncommissioned officers swapping the latest rumors. Private Harrison ushered Fargo to Canby's office, rapped once, and at a command from within, opened the door for him.

The major was at his desk, studying a large map he had spread out on top. "We've heard from Tuck Garson," he said. "He left us this ultimatum." The major handed Fargo a ragged, yellow sheet of paper. On it, written in a surprisingly precise handwriting, was a short message:

> Unless I am paid the sum of two hundred thousand dollars, every Western Union employee between here and the Rockies will be killed, and the telegraph line to California will never be completed. You have one month to have the money sent from the States. In thirty days I will contact you with further instructions. Tuck Garson.

Fargo crumpled the letter in his fist and prepared to ride.

6

A little girl of nine or ten was scampering about in front of a Conestoga, frolicking with a puppy, when Skye Fargo rode up. Over a dozen wagons ringed the clearing beside the Laramie River. The dog barked fiercely, or as fiercely as the small bundle of hair and bones could manage, and the girl dashed under the wagon and peered fearfully up at him.

"Can I help you, m-m-mister?" she stammered.

"Where is everyone else?" Fargo asked. No other emigrants were anywhere to be seen.

"They went to the fort," the girl answered. "Ma said I could stay and play with Abe. But she told me to be careful of strangers." The girl looked him over. "You're not anyone I know, so I reckon that makes you one."

"Yes, but I won't hurt you." Fargo was dismayed her parents could be so careless. Strangers weren't the only danger. Rattlers thrived in these parts, cougars were common, and there was always the chance of a stray hostile or two sneaking in close to the post. "I'm hunting for someone. Maybe you've seen him."

"What does he look like?" the child asked.

"He's a small man, wearing a sombrero."

"A what?"

"A big hat—" Fargo began.

"Oh!" the girl squealed, and came out from underneath the wagon. She had long flaxen hair and a cute button nose. "Is it big and round like this?" She made a wide imaginary circle around her head with her finger.

"That's about right, yes."

"I saw him!" The girl pointed at a gravel bar. "About an hour ago he stopped to let his horse drink." She gnawed her lip a moment. "I didn't like him much. He kept staring at Abe and me. When he left, he smiled and waved but I didn't wave back. He was spooky."

"Thank you," Fargo said and reined the pinto toward the river. "If I were you," he said over a shoulder, "I'd stay in the wagon until your folks get back."

"But Ma said I could play."

"It would be better if you did. Your mother didn't know there are a lot of strangers around today."

"Oh. All right. Thanks, mister. I will."

She was as good as her word. When Fargo reached the gravel bar, the girl was roosting on the seat with her puppy by her side. She grinned and waved, so he did likewise. Then he got down to business.

Fresh tracks confirmed the girl's story.

Fargo followed them. Valdez had forded the Laramie and stopped in a stand of cottonwoods directly across from the wagons. It appeared Valdez's mount had stood there for quite a while. The *pistolero* hadn't climbed down, and the grass showed no evidence of being grazed. So what had Valdez been doing? A cold fury filled Fargo as he stared at the wagons, at the little girl petting her puppy. Then he clucked the Ovaro into motion and resumed tracking.

Valdez had paralleled the Laramie River. Every so often he had stopped, always directly across from emigrant encampments, and always in heavy cover so he couldn't be seen.

Fargo was confident he would overtake the hardcase fairly soon. The girl's guess of an hour tallied with when he had lost sight of Valdez near the fort. He pushed the stallion, holding to a trot once the tracks left the vicinity of the river. At that point the *pistolero* seemed to have headed on a westerly bearing.

Fargo was certain the Mexican had delivered the note from Garson. It had been found tacked to the entrance to the headquarter's building at some point before he had spotted Valdez at the fort.

It was Major Canby's opinion Garson was insane, and Fargo tended to agree. The government would never agree to pay. A massive manhunt would be launched. The military wouldn't rest until Garson was in custody, or dead.

Canby had made another point. It could be that Garson just wanted to stir things up. Maybe General Oliver was right about Garson being a Southern sympathizer sent to sow chaos.

But Fargo wasn't going to let it come to that. He intended to track Valdez to Garson's lair, and if the odds were too great, call in Canby and a detachment of soldiers to eliminate the gang. But if he could catch Garson alone, or with only a few others present, he would take the matter into his own hands.

Killers like Garson and Valdez were a blight on the frontier. They were worse than rabid dogs. Murdering for the warped thrill of it, they didn't care how many innocents they butchered. And they would go on slaughtering until they were six feet under.

In recent years, outlaw ranks west of the Mississippi had swelled. Hellions who refused to live by society's rules flocked to the frontier so they could live as they chose. Hard, cruel men, predators who preyed on the weak and the gullible, desperados who stayed one jump ahead of a noose or prison.

Fargo despised men like Garson. He shared their love of freedom, their dislike of laws and regulations, but he abhorred killing for the sake of killing. Even in the wilderness there had to be some proprieties.

The tracks were bearing to the northwest. It was open country, and Fargo brought the stallion to a gallop and sustained it for as long as was prudent before continuing on. The Mexican had done the same, and Fargo realized that it would take longer to catch up than he thought.

Hours elapsed. The sun began its downward arc, and still there was no sign of Valdez.

The terrain had undergone a change, from grassland to rugged ravines and gullies to sparsely timbered hills. Soon the *pistolero*'s tracks looped to the north, and it occurred to Fargo that the gunman had completed roughly half of a wide circle. If they kept on going as they were, and Valdez eventually turned south, they would end up back in the vicinity of Fort Laramie.

Fargo was tempted to cut directly across country to test his hunch, but if he was wrong, he'd lose half a day or more. He contented himself with sticking to the trail. Severe disappointment set in once it dawned he wouldn't overtake Valdez before dark. The sun was balanced on the western rim of the world, the shadows lengthened, and he was still half an hour behind. The Mexican had a damn good horse.

Twilight descended, and Fargo gave thought to stopping. In a wooded glade beside a shallow stream he finally, unhappily, drew rein. Stripping off the saddle, he spread out his bedroll and made a cold camp. Water and pemmican were his supper.

Once night fell, a bestial chorus serenaded him. Wolves were in full throat. Coyotes yipped with abandon. The grunts of prowling bears and the shrieks of panthers punctuated the vastness at regular intervals.

Fargo decided to turn in early. He needed to be up before sunrise. As he settled under his blankets with his saddle for a pillow, he gazed off through the trees and was startled to spy a flickering pinpoint of light to the south. It was a fire, a small one, and as best Fargo could judge, it was right on his back trail.

Someone was following him.

Siting up, Fargo gauged the distance A mile, perhaps a bit less. Had Valdez somehow looped around behind him? he wondered. Or was it someone else? Garson's outfit, perhaps? Had they lured him into a trap, and aimed to ambush him come morning?

Standing, Fargo hurriedly saddled the pinto and forked leather. The light was a beacon, drawing him unerringly to its source. When he was near enough to distinguish flickering fingers of flame and vague huddled shapes, he halted and cautiously advanced on foot, the Henry at the ready.

Voices reached him, not clearly, but clear enough for Fargo to glean the language wasn't English. When he was a hundred yards out, he flattened. Exercising the utmost caution, he crept close enough to learn who they were. He was surprised when it wasn't who he figured it would be.

Seven painted warriors were spaced around the fire, some squatting, some seated, all talking in low tones. The style of their hair, their buckskins, their moccasins, identified them as Oglala Sioux.

Fargo had stumbled upon the war party mentioned by Major Canby, who were harassing emigrants up and down the trail. They were all young, in their early twenties, if that, which struck Fargo as odd. Usually it was the older warriors who organized and led raids. Either the seven had split off from a larger group, or they were a bunch of overeager youngsters out to make a name for themselves.

The Sioux were a warrior society. Deeds of valor were highly esteemed. Those who performed the most courageous acts and those who counted the most coup rose to positions of prominence. It was every young man's dream to one day be a great warrior others looked up to. To that end, they risked life and limb on raids against enemy villages, or against whites.

Fargo crawled closer. No doubt the seven Oglalas assumed a lone white man would be easy pickings, and had it in mind to ambush him the next day. But their inexperience was showing. First off, they had camped on an open slope instead of in the trees where their fire was less likely to be spotted. Second, they had tied their horses but had not hobbled them, which made it easy to run the animals off. As Fargo was about to do. Left afoot, the warriors would have no choice but to head home.

The mounts were by some pines. Fargo snaked toward

them, never letting his gaze stray from the Oglalas. He crawled to within half a dozen yards of the horses before he realized there were *eight,* not seven.

One of the warriors was unaccounted for.

Rising up onto his elbows, Fargo scoured the clearing. He swiveled toward a clump of brush to his right. Just as he saw a dark figure off in the near distance, he heard a metallic click. In reflex, he threw himself to one side.

The night resounded to the boom of a rifle. Lead kicked up dirt within six inches of Fargo's face. He had hoped to avoid spilling blood, but when the figure bounded toward him and a rifle lever rasped, he did what was necessary. He raised the Henry and fired from the hip.

The Oglala was hurled backward as if kicked by a mule.

Whoops of outrage pealed out as Fargo rolled up into a crouch. The other Sioux had leaped to their feet and were rushing toward him, some armed with rifles, some with bows, one husky warrior carried a lance. War clubs and knives were also in evidence.

Fargo spoke the Sioux tongue fluently. For a brief instant he considered shouting to let them know he meant no harm. But it would be pointless when one of their own was thrashing about and howling in agony. Either he battled them, or he ran. He chose flight.

Guns spat flame and hot lead as Fargo bolted toward the pines. He was almost to the undergrowth when a bullet nipped his shoulder, tearing the buckskin but not penetrating his flesh. Whirling, he banged out two swift shots to discourage pursuit, then raced off into the trees.

Fargo had to get out of there and back to the Ovaro. But if he headed north, the war party might spot the stallion before he reached it and bring the pinto down in a hail of gunfire to keep him from escaping. So to lead them astray, he ran south instead, deliberately making more noise than he ordinarily would. The ruse worked. Five or six warriors flew after him. The others knelt beside their fallen friend.

Mentally cursing his luck, Fargo poured on the speed. But he couldn't go as fast as he would like, not in the dark, not when a misstep would reap disaster. Logs and other obstacles hove out of the night without warning, and he had to stay alert.

The Oglalas were shouting to one another. "Spread out!" one hollered. "But not too far apart so he can not elude us."

"Did you get a good look at him, Antelope Horn?" another cried. "Is it a blue coat?"

"Blue coats always hunt in packs, like wolves," Antelope Horn responded. "This is just one man. Now be quiet and find him."

The woods in Fargo's wake became quiet. Halting, he crouched behind a boulder. He would never have guessed had he not known, that half a dozen men were out there seeking his life. They moved like ghosts, making no more sound than the breeze made.

Fargo continued south another fifty yards. Deeming it far enough, he bore to the east. A large log provided the hiding place he needed. Lying on his stomach, he pressed against it and waited.

It wasn't long before furtive movement gave the warriors away. They were on either side, strung out in a line.

Fargo tensed at the scrape of a moccasin on pine needles. Moving only his eyes, he peered to the right. An inky silhouette was slinking by within ten feet of the log, an Oglala with a bow, an arrow nocked to the sinew string.

Fargo scarcely breathed. Beyond the bowman other forms moved, gliding past. When they were out of earshot, Fargo grinned and carefully rose. He had given them the slip. Now he could sneak back to the pinto and leave.

Turning, Fargo took a single step. Abruptly out of the murk flew the husky warrior with the lance. A tapered tip sheared at Fargo's chest, seeking out his heart as he nimbly skipped aside. The Oglala pressed the attack, the lance arcing at his abdomen, and Fargo bounded backward, a thrust of the Henry's stock blocking the blow. Instantly, the warrior shifted and drove the lance at Fargo's neck. Another swing of the rifle countered it.

Moving in close, Fargo hammered the butt against the Sioux's jaw. Once, then twice, and the man buckled to his knees.

Fargo whirled to run, but strong arms wrapped around his legs and he was borne to earth. Twisting, he elbowed the Oglala in the mouth as the man raised the lance once more. It slowed the warrior but didn't stop him.

A wrench of Fargo's neck saved his life. Missing by a whisker, the lance thudded into the earth. Before the young Oglala could try again, Fargo whipped the Henry up and back, the barrel connecting with the man's temple.

Dazed, the warrior keeled over onto his side.

Fargo vaulted erect and ran. The commotion was bound to bring the others. So much for escaping unnoticed. He saw the fire ahead, saw two Oglalas helping the wounded man toward it, and he veered to the left to avoid them. But one of them caught sight of him, let go of the wounded warrior, and flew to head him off.

To the rear, war whoops arose.

"This way!" Antelope Horn shouted. "He is over here!"

Brush crackled close behind, and Fargo glanced back. A benighted apparition was bounding toward him like a bloodhound hot on his scent.

Swiveling at the hips, Fargo squeezed off a shot on the fly. The man to his rear toppled, but another figure was there to take his place.

"Here! Over here!"

Fargo barreled on. Something whizzed past his neck and he heard an arrow thud into a tree. Seconds later a second arrow nearly clipped his arm. But he didn't dare return fire, not when the Oglala in front of him was almost on top of him. Extending the Henry, he sighted on the center of the onrushing black mass. And tripped.

Fargo couldn't say whether it was an exposed root or

a rock. Whatever the cause, his foot snagged, and he was pitched onto his face just as he squeezed the trigger. The slug plowed into the earth instead of into the Oglala.

In the next second the warrior was there, an arrow notched to a bow. He had waited until he was so close he couldn't possibly miss. And now he released the shaft.

Fargo frantically rolled to the right as the string twanged. He felt a jolt to his sleeve but no pain. Pushing onto a knee, he saw the man already notching another arrow. Automatically, Fargo's hand dipped to his Colt. He fired as the Sioux took aim, firing again as the man staggered and fell, letting go of the drawstring. The arrow flew toward him, passing within a hair's breadth of his cheek.

Hurtling on past, Fargo holstered the Colt and pumped his legs for all they were worth. Moccasins pounded to his rear again. A tall Oglala was closing swiftly. The man had a rifle, but he made no attempt to employ it, a clue he wanted to take Fargo alive.

The horses were just ahead, prancing and nickering and pulling at the ropes that tethered them. It wouldn't take much to send them into a panic.

Spinning, Fargo buried the Henry's stock into the tall warrior's gut as the man was about to seize him.

The other Oglala by the fire was elevating a bow.

Fargo ignored him and faced the horses. Working the Henry, he banged lead into the ground and let out with a screech that would do justice to a catamount. The effect was exactly as he desired.

Whinnying and rearing, the war horses broke loose and stampeded, all except for a magnificent chestnut.

Lunging at the picket, Fargo sought to scare it off, too, but the whiz of an arrow impressed on him not to press his luck more than he already had. Snapping a shot at the Oglala with the bow, he sped northward.

Only two warriors were still in pursuit, their lithe forms flowing through the high grass like a pair of tawny cougars, whooping and yipping.

Fargo didn't try to shoot them. He wanted to avoid spilling more blood, but he might be forced to, as the Oglalas were clearly out for his. His boots flying, he dashed toward a whitish patch starkly outlined against the backdrop of the night. It was the white band that marked his pinto from back to belly.

The loud panting of the two warriors grew louder. They were gaining. Not much, but enough that Fargo wouldn't be able to climb on the Ovaro and ride off before they reached him. Since he couldn't avoid them, he had to confront them. And to that end, he did the unexpected.

Suddenly stopping, Fargo rotated. The first Oglala was mere yards away, coming too fast to stop. Fargo swung the Henry as if it were a club and the blow lifted the man clear out of his moccasins.

The second warrior had a war club. As Fargo pivoted, the Oglala swung at his legs, aiming for his knees, seeking to cripple him. Flinging himself to the right, Fargo saved himself, but it left him momentarily off balance, and before he could recover, the Oglala swung again.

Exquisite torment speared Fargo's ribs. Jolted, he stumbled and would have gone down had he not used the Henry as a crutch. His head swimming, he looked up to see the Oglala about to swing a third time. There would be no avoiding it.

Again Fargo resorted to the Colt. Again it leaped into his hand and flashed thunder. He shot the warrior in the shoulder, thinking that would be enough, but although the man fell to one knee, in the next heartbeat he was up again and hefting the war club overhead.

Fargo triggered the Colt once more, aiming lower. Then he whirled and hooked his boot in a stirrup. War whoops rent the woodland as he painfully pulled himself into the saddle and reined to the north.

Rifles cracked. Two shots. Three. Four.

With a slap of Fargo's legs, the Ovaro galloped off. He bent low to make it harder for the Oglalas to hit him, hoping all the while the stallion didn't take a stray bullet. Only after the whoops faded on the wind did he straighten, grimacing at the pain it provoked.

Fargo was worried a rib or two was busted. Pressing his elbow to his left side, he rode until he was back where he had started, in the glade by the shallow stream. Sliding off, he had to grit his teeth to keep from crying out.

There was no sign of pursuit, but Fargo stood and listened for a full ten minutes before he accepted the fact. His side was throbbing. Stepping to the steam, he hunkered and tugged at his buckskin shirt, raising it high enough to examine his chest. Even in the dark, the discolored skin was apparent. He'd have a nasty bruise in the morning. Gingerly, he probed with his fingertips. He was in acute misery and his side was swelling up, but his ribs seemed intact.

Leaning down, Fargo cupped cold water and applied it to his side, shivering when some trickled below his belt. He kept pouring water on himself until the pangs subsided enough for him to stand and walk to the pinto.

Removing his saddle taxed his self-control. Every movement, however slight, spiked sharp pangs. He laid out his blankets, then sat propped against his saddle, mulling over the turn of events.

Fargo wouldn't let a little pain, or even a lot, deter him from tracking Valdez down. Come morning, he would push on, and he would push on hard in order to catch up to the *pistolero*. Stopping Garson was all that counted. He could live with the discomfort. When it was over, he would head to Denver to recuperate and treat himself to a week or two of gambling and the willing company of a few lovely doves.

Recalling that he hadn't reloaded, Fargo laid the Henry and the Colt next to him and corrected his oversight. It hurt every time he raised his left arm higher than his waist. And when he reached behind him to slide a cartridge from his gun belt, it felt as if someone had buried a dagger in his side.

Finished, Fargo sank down to try and sleep. He lay

on his back gazing at the Big Dipper, waiting for drowsiness to claim him. But it wouldn't. His mind was racing, his nerves still on edge. To amuse himself, he tried counting buffalo instead of sheep, but after counting to one hundred and forty, he gave it up and switched to counting scantily clad ladies of the night. Even that didn't work.

Exasperated, Fargo sat up, moving too quickly. He paid for it when his ribs protested. Clutching his side, he doubled over.

To the northwest a wolf gave voice to a lonesome lament and was answered by another to the east. Presently five or six were howling in unison, filling the night with their clamor.

Fargo rose and moved stiffly toward the stream. More cold water was called for, enough to soothe the pain and quell the throbbing long enough for him to fall asleep. As it was, he faced the prospect of being up most of the night, which would leave him in no shape to tangle with the likes of Tuck Garson.

Kneeling, Fargo pried at his shirt, then dipped his hand into the water. As the howling faded he thought he heard a hoofbeat. Cocking his head, he tried to verify whether he really had heard it or whether his imagination was to blame, but the wolves started up again, their howls rolling off across the foothills like the eerie lament of disembodied spirits.

Thinking he must be mistaken, Fargo splashed water on himself. Goosebumps broke out, and soon a chill came over him, but bit by bit the hurt lessened. Not as much as he would like, though.

Soon the lupine choir ended their song.

Fargo lowered his hand for the umpteenth time, then went rigid as another hoofbeat thumped dully in the darkness. Forgetting himself, he spun. So did the glade as newfound agony rocked him and dizziness assailed his senses.

To the south a figure appeared, a man on horseback, slowly, warily approaching. It had to be an Oglala.

Remembering the fine chestnut war horse that hadn't run off, Fargo moved to the right, into a deep shadow created by several closely spaced firs. It was just one warrior, he assured himself. Despite the shape he was in, he should be able to handle things without having to kill again.

The rider reined up twenty-five feet out. Dismounting, he stalked soundlessly forward.

Fargo dropped his right hand to palm his Colt, but his fingers closed on empty air. Shocked, he glanced at his blankets. He had left the Colt and the Henry lying on them after he had reloaded!

7

The pounding pain was to blame. Skye Fargo had made a mistake only the greenest of greenhorns would make, an oversight that might cost him his life. He took a step toward his bedroll, then stopped. It wouldn't be smart to compound his first blunder by making another. The Oglala was bound to spot him and would drop him before he got halfway there.

Squatting, Fargo ran a hand over the ground, searching for something he could use as a weapon. A rock, a downed tree limb, anything. But all he found were a few small stones. Selecting one, he scooped up a handful of loose dirt with his other hand.

The Oglala took his sweet time. Bent low, he moved from tree to tree, crouching behind each a while before going to the next.

Fargo's luck hadn't entirely deserted him. Stooped over as the warrior was, the man couldn't tell his blankets were empty. His saddle was in the way.

The Ovaro was aware of the Sioux but had not whinnied in alarm. It was watching him, its ears pricked. When the man was almost to the glade, the stallion glanced at the fir Fargo was behind and stomped a hoof.

The Oglala stopped dead. He didn't move for a long time, except for his head swinging from side to side. At last he crept into the open, his knees bent, holding a bow with the string drawn.

Fargo braced himself for what he must do. Another few feet and the warrior would realize no one was there. The Oglala was bound to spot the rifle and the pistol, and if he got his hands on them, Fargo was as good as dead.

The warrior sidled one foot forward, then carefully moved the other. He started to unfurl, rising, and sighting down the arrow at the blankets. Not quite upright, he froze, staring at the flat bedroll in bewilderment.

It was the moment Fargo had been waiting for. He threw the stone with all his might, off to the left, well past the Ovaro. It crashed into the brush, making more noise than Fargo dared hope, and the Oglala spun toward the sound.

Instantly, Fargo charged, his teeth clenched against the agony. He was only six or seven feet from the warrior when the man heard him and turned, directly into the handful of dirt Fargo flung into his eyes.

Blinded, the Oglala stumbled backward. The bowstring twanged, the arrow imbedding itself in the soil.

Fargo never broke stride. Lowering his right shoulder, he slammed into the Sioux like a battering ram, bowling the Oglala over. Fargo nearly went down, too, as overwhelming waves of pulsating torment racked him. Dazed, barely able to focus, he teetered to the blankets and snatched the Colt.

The young warrior, frantically rubbing his eyes, had dropped the bow and drawn a hunting knife. Blinking furiously, he took a step forward.

"Stop where you are," Fargo said in the Sioux language. "Any closer and I will kill you." To accent his point, he curled back the hammer.

The Oglala halted, still blinking in an effort to clear his vision, his eyes and cheeks smeared with dirt and tears.

"Drop the knife," Fargo said.

The young man did no such thing. Scowling, he raised his arm and tensed to make a desperate spring.

"You will never reach me," Fargo said. "But throw your life away if you want." He extended the revolver. "Your choice."

The Oglala's bronzed face contorted in simmering rage. Releasing the bone-handled weapon, he glared like

79

a beast at bay. "Who are you, white cur, that you speak the tongue of my people?"

"Once, many winters ago, I lived among the Minniconjou," Fargo disclosed. "I am a friend to all Dakotas."

"A friend?" the warrior spat. "You attacked us! You shot some of us! One man has died."

"I am sorry about that, but they were trying to kill me," Fargo said. "All I wanted to do was scare off your horses."

"So you claim." The Oglala thumped his chest with a fist. "I am Antelope Horn. Kill me now, or I will eventually hunt you down no matter how long it takes."

Fargo wasn't inclined to debate the point. His chest was splitting. His head hammered. Sidestepping to his saddle, he grabbed his coiled rope and pointed with it. "Walk toward those trees. No sudden moves or I will shoot."

Antelope Horn backed off, staring at the lariat. "What do you plan to do?"

"Protect you from yourself." Fargo spied a suitable trunk and pointed again. "Take off your quiver and sit with your back against that tree."

The Oglala suspected treachery. He slowly sank down, hatred rife on his features, his jaw muscles twitching in rage.

Fargo eased onto a knee and placed the rope on the ground. Covering Antelope Horn, he uncoiled it, then tossed an end to the warrior. "Loop this around the tree and yourself three times. Then place your hands behind the tree."

Antelope Horn obeyed, but he didn't like it. When he was done he glowered balefully, his urge to kill as plain as the war paint on his face.

Circling partway around the trunk, Fargo pressed the Colt's muzzle against the warrior's head to insure Antelope Horn didn't try anything. With his left hand he tightened the rope enough so that the Oglala couldn't move his arms. Twirling the revolver into his holster, he tightened the rope even more. Three sturdy knots insured Antelope Horn would stay there. Satisfied, he stepped back.

"What will you do now?" Antelope Horn asked. "Torture me, as your kind did to my sister and the others?"

"What are you talking about?" Fargo said, squatting. The pain was subsiding somewhat, but he still found it difficult to think clearly through the dull ache.

"One moon ago, by the Sweetgrass. My sister and three other girls were off gathering roots and berries." Antelope Horn darkened, his hatred terrible to behold. "White men found them. White men, and two others. They dragged the girls off. They—" He stopped, his whole body quaking violently.

"The whites killed them?"

"Yes!" Antelope Horn snarled. "But they tortured them first. They ripped out my sister's tongue. They cut off her nose and her ears. After they had their way with her." His voice broke, and he sucked in deep breaths, trying not to weep.

"You will not believe this, but you have my sympathy," Fargo said. He understood now why Antelope Horn's band had been harassing wagon trains, and why all the warriors were young. "You have been searching for those responsible ever since."

Antelope Horn was too choked with emotion to do more than grunt.

"The warriors with you are brothers and relatives of the women who were killed. And you left your village without waiting for the elders to sit in council."

Again the young Oglala grunted.

"But how did you hope to find those responsible?"

Clearing his throat, Antelope Horn said, "One of the girls lived long enough to describe them. There were eight, plus the other two."

"Who are these other two you keep mentioning?"

"A part-Pawnee breed and a Mexican."

Pawnee Tom and Valdez. An icy sensation filled Fargo, as if he had been standing naked in deep snow for hours on end. "What did she say about the white men involved?"

"One was big and wore a buffalo coat. Another had a black vest. Two whites wore long coats and had beards."

In his mind's eye, Fargo pictured Angus Stark, Brody, and the Baxter brothers. "I know of these men. They are bad medicine. I have been sent to find them. When I do, they will pay for the lives they have taken."

"A white man sent to kill his own kind?" Antelope Horn didn't believe it.

"They have tortured and killed many whites, as well as Indians," Fargo said. "They must be stopped no matter what." He paused. "I have already killed one of them. I also shot the man with the black vest but he might still be alive."

Antelope Horn digested the news.

"Had I known about your sister and the other women," Fargo went on, "I would not have tried to run off your horses. The blue coats told me you had been causing trouble."

"When we first started hunting for the killers, we tried to tell the whites we met what had happened. But they did not understand us. They were scared of us, and thought we meant to harm them. After a while I stopped trying to explain." Antelope Horn's rage was fading. "You are the first white we have met who speaks our tongue. How are you known?"

"The whites call me Skye Fargo." He spoke his name in English since there was no Sioux equivalent. "To the Minniconjou, the Shoshones, the Cheyennes, and others, I am known by different names."

"What do you do?"

"I am a tracker, a scout. When the blue coats need someone to follow sign where others cannot, they call on me. When whites need a guide through country they have never set foot in, they ask me to lead them. They have a name for me that means 'one who never loses the trail.' "

"Then that is what I will call you," Antelope Horn said. "Never Loses the Trail."

"I am sorry about the misunderstanding," Fargo said, sincerely. "Your friends will be out for my blood, and I can't blame them."

"Not if I tell them what you have told me," Antelope Horn said. "That is, if you let me live."

Rising, Fargo walked to the tree and untied the knots. "Take your weapons and go. I will not try to stop you."

Uncertainly, expecting a ruse, Antelope Horn shed the coils and stepped up out of them. Never taking his eyes off Fargo, he retrieved the bone-handled knife, slung the quiver over his back, and picked up the bow.

"Go in peace," Fargo said. "When I catch the killers, I will remember your sister, and I will show no mercy."

Antelope Horn seemed to want to say something, but instead he pivoted and hastened to the chestnut. Swinging lithely astride it, he reined the animal around and departed at a hard gallop.

Fargo was taking a tremendous chance. The young Oglala might return in the dead of night to slit his throat while he slept. To be safe, he rolled up his bedroll, reattached the rope to his saddle, and, leading the pinto, carried his personal effects into the trees. When he had gone a hundred yards he hitched the stallion to a low limb and wearily sank to the ground.

Curling up on his uninjured side, Fargo waited for sleep to claim him. This time it did so almost immediately, and he drifted into deep slumber, sleeping so soundly he did something he hadn't done in years: he slept past sunrise.

Light dappling his face awakened him. Without thinking, Fargo sat up. His ribs screamed in protest and pain spiked through him. Pressing his arms to his chest, he sat still until the pangs were gone. Then, looking up, he received a worse shock than he had the night before when he left his guns lying on his blanket.

Perched on a log fifteen feet away were Antelope Horn and another young Oglala, a stocky warrior with a pie-pan face and ruddy cheeks. Antelope Horn's bow was in his lap. The other warrior had an old Sharps, the stock studded with brass tacks, resting across his thighs.

"How long have you been there?" Fargo asked, upset he hadn't heard them. They could have slain him with ease.

"Since before the first birds sang," Antelope Horn said. "Are you badly hurt? You groaned often."

"I am fine," Fargo said. But the spasm that lanced through him when he moved to stand made a liar of him. Finally succeeding in standing erect, he put his hand on the pinto to steady himself. "To what do I owe this visit?"

"You are tracking the killers of my sister."

"I have said so, yes."

Antelope Horn smiled. "We want to help you. This is High Bull. He has counted coup on the Blackfeet."

"I am sure you are both brave men," Fargo said, "but I hunt alone. I would not let the blue coats come. And I will not let you."

Antelope Horn and High Bull exchanged glances. "You refuse our help?" Antelope Horn said. "After what I told you? Have you never lost someone you loved? Someone who filled your heart with happiness?"

Memories Fargo had long suppressed washed over him. "I have lost loved ones," he admitted.

"Then how can you say no? It was my *sister* they cut up, Never Loses the Trail. She was a kind girl. Always cheerful. Always smiling. Always willing to help anyone who needed it. Just to know her was to know happiness." Antelope Horn's voice dripped misery. "Can you imagine what it was like for her at the end? To have those men abuse her? To have them do the things they did? How she must have suffered?"

"I can imagine," Fargo said more gruffly than he intended.

High Bull addressed him. "I do not like whites. But Antelope Horn says you are our friend and he never lies." The stocky Oglala paused. "My cousin was one of those who were butchered. They tore her fingernails from her fingers, and gouged out her eyes with a burning stick. I want these men dead. I will not rest until they are."

"I do not blame you," Fargo allowed.

"Then let us go with you," Antelope Horn said. "You are hurt, and they are many." He rose. "We promise to do as you say."

"In all things? Both of you?"

High Bull also stood. "I give you my word, Never Loses the Trail. Permit us to fight at your side and we will be your brothers for life."

Fargo believed they were in earnest, but he had grave reservations. There was no guarantee any of them would come out of it alive. But he couldn't deny that no one had a better right to tag along than they did. "I hunt alone," he repeated as their faces became crestfallen, "but I am willing to make an exception."

The young warriors grinned.

"Only so long as you are true to your promise to do as I tell you," Fargo stressed.

"Agreed," Antelope Horn said.

Beyond the pair were a couple of war horses, the chestnut and another. Which reminded Fargo. "What about your friends? How will they fare without you?"

Antelope Horn answered. "Four of our horses came back. We made a travois for the wounded, and they will return to our village."

"We talked it over," High Bull said, "and we bear you no ill will."

Were they on the level? Fargo wondered. The Sioux could be devious when they wanted to be. It was entirely possible Antelope Horn and High Bull were merely playing along, and after Garson's bunch had been dealt with, they would turn on him.

As the old saying went, Fargo would cross that bridge when he came to it.

The sun was half an hour into the sky. Anxious to head out, Fargo bent to lift his saddle blanket. His ribs were stiff and his body was so sore he was barely able to do it. But he did, and then lifted his shirt to examine himself in the light of day.

"A war club did that?" Antelope Horn asked.

Fargo nodded. His left side was horribly discolored, the skin black and blue from his sternum to the bottom of his rib cage. His side was swollen and puffy. Lower down, he was extremely sensitive to the touch. He still didn't think his ribs were broken, but the pain spoke otherwise.

"Can you ride?" High Bull inquired.

"Let's find out." Fargo gripped the saddle, took a deep breath, and swung up and over the pinto. For a second he thought he would black out, but the feeling faded. The more he moved about, the less it bothered him. Within five minutes he was ready.

The Oglalas mounted up.

With Fargo in the lead, they rode to where he had stopped tracking the previous evening and picked up the *pistolero*'s trail. It continued eastward, but by noon the tracks were bearing to the south, exactly as Fargo had foretold. Valdez had ridden in a loop and was returning to Fort Laramie.

It made no sense.

An hour later, as they neared a string of low hills, Fargo spied wispy tendrils of smoke curling skyward. The Oglalas saw it a second later.

"We have found them!" Antelope Horn exclaimed.

High Bull started to goad his mount past the Ovaro. "The white devil in the buffalo coat is mine!"

Fargo wheeled the pinto to prevent the warrior from going any further. "You gave your word to do this my way," he reminded them. "I will go on ahead and make sure it is the ones we are after. If it is, I will signal you. Then, and only then, will you avenge your loved ones."

"Very well," High Bull said. "But do not take too long. My blood boils for the scalps of these killers."

With a flick of the reins, Fargo trotted toward a gully. Its sides were high enough to screen him from unfriendly eyes, and it wound in among the hills in the direction he had to go. Shucking the Henry from its scabbard, he fed a cartridge into the chamber.

The bottom of the gully was littered with gravel. As a result, the clatter of the pinto's hooves was louder than Fargo liked. He slowed to a walk and tried to avoid the gravel as much as possible.

Presently a hill loomed on his left. From behind it rose the smoke, curling lazily on the sluggish breeze.

Stopping, Fargo slid down and climbed to the top of the gully. Scrub brush and boulders sprinkled the hill, enough for him to gain the crest undetected. His ribs ached abominably, but he shut out the pain and did what he had to. He eeled the last few yards on his elbows and knees, removed his hat, and cautiously took a look-see.

He had struck pay dirt. Camped in a grassy vale nourished by a small spring were eight men. Five he recognized: Angus Stark, Valdez, Dallas, and the Baxter brothers. The remaining four were cut from the same coarse cloth. Two were lanky range wolves, the third a man built like a wild boar, the last a gunman with a goatee.

Coffee was brewing in a pot on a small fire. A gutted buck lay nearby, being sliced up by the gunman with the goatee and the Baxter brothers. Ten horses were picketed near the spring.

Spares, Fargo figured. He saw no sign of Frank Brody. Either the two-gun killer had died after all, or he was still laid up back at Honest Jack's Emporium.

Sliding the Henry forward, Fargo wedged it to his shoulder and took deliberate aim. He had promised the Oglalas he would signal them, but he had a clear shot at the man he believed was Tuck Garson and he couldn't pass it up. Garson was the glue that held the gang together. Without him, they would drift apart.

Fixing the front sight on Angus Stark's chest, Fargo aligned the rear sight with the front and lightly applied his forefinger to the trigger. Stark had to be Garson. The comments Valdez had made that night on the North Platte, and Stark's lack of concern when Brody and

Pawnee Tom were gunned down, pointed to him being the cold-blooded beast everyone was after.

Stark was seated on a flat rock, talking to Dallas and Valdez. He seemed to be arguing with the *pistolero*. Suddenly the Mexican jumped up and slapped the buffalo hunter across the face.

Fargo raised his cheek from the Henry, awaiting the explosion sure to ensue. To his amazement, Stark didn't do a thing. Fargo's conviction he had the right man evaporated like mist under a burning sun.

"Enjoying the view, are you, young man?"

Fargo swung around, or tried to, only to find himself staring into the muzzles of two rifles. One was held by a gray-haired pilgrim almost as old as George Melton, his bony frame clothed in a flannel shirt and overalls. The other man was another half-breed with the flat, lifeless eyes of a sidewinder.

"It would please me greatly if you would lie there and not move," the older fellow said. "If you do, I'm afraid my associate and I will make worm food of you." He gestured at his "associate." "Honta, do the honors."

Fargo was fit to be tied. At their mercy, he had to lie there as the one called Honta relieved him of the Henry and the Colt.

"Now then," the old man said, smiling. "Allow me to introduce myself. My name is Tuck Garson."

"You're—!" Fargo blurted in astonishment, then caught himself. But the harm had been done, and the old man's smile widened.

"Ah. I see you have heard of me."

Fargo was dumbfounded. The terror of the plains was as ordinary and harmless looking as a kitten. If he passed the old man on a city street, he wouldn't give him a second glance.

"Be so good as to explain who you are and what you are doing here," Tuck Garson said in his overly civil manner.

"I'm here to join your gang," Fargo said. It was the first thing that popped into his head, and the one lie that might buy him precious minutes of life.

"You don't say?" Garson's light-blue eyes danced with merriment. "And I'm supposed to be gullible enough to believe you, is that it?"

"Why wouldn't you?" Fargo said.

"Well, for one thing, you were about to pick off one of my men. For another, I have a knack for telling what people are like just by looking at them. And you, stranger, weren't molded from the same clay as those boys down below." Garson motioned. "On your feet. I'm sure they'll want to make your acquaintance."

Honta gouged his rifle against the small of Fargo's back as they walked down the slope. At the spring, Stark and the others leaped to their feet and rushed to the bottom, some brandishing hardware.

"That's the jasper we were tellin' you about, boss," the big buffalo hunter said. "The bastard who outgunned Brody and Pawnee Tom."

"I suspected as much," Tuck Garson said. "He fit your description." Garson moved around in front of Fargo and lowered his Spencer. "How is it that you show up here, in the middle of nowhere, right where we happen to be? Coincidence? I think not." He glanced at the *pistolero*. "Valdez?"

"Señor?"

"Maybe you can answer that question."

"Me?" Valdez laughed as if it were a great joke. "How would I know?"

"The only way he could have found us was if he tracked you here. Yet I specifically told you to watch your back trail. Is there anything you would like to say to justify your lapse in judgement?"

Valdez took exception. "I do not like being called stupid, señor. I did as you told me. There is no proof this hombre followed me."

"I don't need to prove it," Garson said. "I know it." And with that, the gray-haired man with the kindly expression, who was old enough to be Fargo's grandfather, leveled the Spencer and fired at point-blank range into the Mexican's face.

8

Skye Fargo had run into all types of killers in his travels. Gunmen, gamblers, paid assassins, renegades, outlaws, outcasts, and hostiles, he had encountered them all at one time or another. Men with no morals or scruples. Men with no compunctions about taking human life. But few impressed him like Tuck Garson, whose kindly, crinkly features showed no anger or resentment or bloodlust. Garson shot Valdez down as nonchalantly as if he were swatting a gnat. And it was that, more than the deed itself, that impressed Fargo, that told him Garson wasn't a run-of-the-mill bad man.

The other cutthroats were riveted in place, some too stupefied to say anything, others trying to hide resentment or disgust. No one, Fargo noticed, objected. No one spoke in the *pistolero*'s behalf.

Garson stared at the ruin he had made of Valdez's face. Still wearing his grandfatherly smile, he fed a new cartridge into the Spencer, then turned to Honta. "Would you please attend to the body? Strip it of anything we can use, of course, as usual."

The half-breed nodded, handed Fargo's guns to Angus Stark, and dragged the Mexican off by the legs.

"Now then," Garson said, pointing the rifle at Fargo, "you did track him here, didn't you?"

"Yes," Fargo said. Lying would serve no useful purpose, and would most likely earn him a grave beside the Mexican.

"The army sent you?"

Again Fargo admitted the truth. "How did you guess?"

The old man's pleasant smile widened. "Oh, please. It hardly takes a genius to discern the obvious. The only other reason for you to have followed the late Mr. Valdez here is to join up with me. But you're not a seasoned killer. Angus told me how you came to the defense of those two boys at Honest Jack's."

"So now you'll gun me down too, is that it?" Fargo bunched his leg muscles to spring. He didn't stand a prayer, but he would go down fighting.

"The thought has crossed my mind," Garson said, "but you're much too valuable to me at the moment. I trust you won't be too disappointed if I let you live."

"I'm valuable to you? How?"

"In due time, sir. In due time." Garson glanced at the Baxter brothers. "One of you fetch a rope and bind our guest's wrists behind his back. We don't want him to do anything foolish."

Both brothers ran toward the horses.

Tuck Garson chuckled. "Did you see that? Ask one to do something and they both do it. They're inseparable, almost as if they were joined at the hip. If I ever have to shoot one, I suppose I'll have to shoot the other, too, just on general principle."

Dallas, the gunman from Texas, had stepped over to the *pistolero*'s prone form. His thumbs hooked in his gun belt, he said, "Mind if I say my piece?"

"Not at all," Garson said. "All of you are free to express your opinions whenever you like. It's not gumption I loathe. It's stupidity."

"Well then, what you just did was wrong. Sure, Valdez was careless. But blowing out his wick was more than he deserved."

"He was your partner, wasn't he?" Garson asked, and didn't wait for an answer. "The two of you rode all the way up here from San Antonio, so it's only natural for you to be upset. But put yourself in my boots. What if an entire company of soldiers had followed him instead of just one tracker? Where would we be right now? I'll tell you. Dead, or in federal custody."

"You're probably right," Dallas conceded. "But like you said, he was my pard. Couldn't you have shot him in the foot instead?"

A note of resentment tinged Garson's reply. "If you'll recall, when the two of you threw in with me I made my demands plain. All of you are to do exactly as I say when I say it, no questions asked. And you were standing right beside Valdez the other day when I gave him instructions on how to deliver the note." Garson paused. "Did I or did I not advise him to check his back trail every hour or so to insure he wasn't being trailed?"

"You did," Dallas said begrudgingly.

"There you have it. By not doing as he was directed, he endangered us all. And a man that careless is bound to be careless again. I did all of us a favor by disposing of him."

Dallas clammed up, but Fargo was willing to bet every dollar he had that the Texan didn't agree. If there was one thing he had learned about Texans, it was that they were fiercely loyal to their friends. They also harbored grudges like most people hoarded wealth. Garson might not realize it, but the matter wasn't settled, not by a long shot.

The Baxter brothers returned bearing a rope. One produced a folding knife and cut off enough to bind Fargo's wrists.

When they were done, Tuck Garson finally lowered the Spencer. "What say I treat you to coffee? Do you have a name or are you unsociable by nature?"

Fargo considered giving a false one. But there was a chance Garson already knew, or suspected. Notoriety had its price, not the least of which was being recognized at the most inopportune moments. So he fessed up.

Angus Stark whistled.

The gunman with the goatee exclaimed, "I'll be damned!"

Tuck Garson nodded knowingly. "Manna from

heaven, boys," he said. "Now the army will have to believe us, won't they?"

Stark chortled. "Hell, I hadn't thought of that, boss! It's better than sending them another note."

"Isn't it, though?" Garson said, and gestured toward the spring. "After you, Mr. Fargo. I suspect you have a hundred and one questions you want to ask, and we might as well relax while we're talking. As for the rest of you—" Garson waved a hand in dismissal "— go on with what you were doing. Except for Mr. Stark."

"I want in on this, too," Dallas said.

"If you like," Garson said amiably.

Fargo was beginning to notice something. Tuck Garson never *stopped* smiling, never wore any other expression than a friendly one. He smiled as he talked, smiled as he walked, and he had smiled as he blew Valdez's head half off. It was unnatural, almost inhuman. And it grated on his nerves.

"Here will do," the butcher announced, indicating a patch of grass bordering the spring.

Fargo sat cross-legged with his back to the pool, his hands inches from the water. He was careful not to let his right pant leg slide up past his boot. Someone might notice the sheath strapped to his ankle.

Garson set the Spencer aside and leaned back. "Where would you like to begin?"

"You're not what I expected."

"You don't say," Garson said. "If I had a dollar for every time someone told me that, I wouldn't need the two hundred thousand dollars the government will be giving me before too long."

Fargo wasn't one to mince words. "You're loco if you think they will. They have patrols out looking for you, and sooner or later one of them will find you. You won't live out the year."

"Hunting for me and finding me are two different things," Garson said. "There's plenty of wide-open space for me to hide in. But let's say they do. Let's say a patrol spots me. They won't lift a finger against us."

"I admire a man with confidence," Fargo baited him.

"On the contrary. I know something you don't. Three or four days from now my men and I will be untouchable."

The big buffalo hunter chortled. "The boss has it all worked out, mister. He's as smart as a fox."

"Why, thank you, Mr. Stark," Garson said with mock humility. "A misspent childhood is to blame. Rather than go outdoors to play and act the fool, I whiled away my hours reading and learning. And it has paid off handsomely. Or will, very shortly."

"I can't wait," Stark said, excitedly rubbing his palms. "Ten thousand dollars is a lot of money. More than I've ever had, more than I've ever *seen*."

Garson looked at Fargo. "It's his share of the take. I get half. The rest divide up the remainder."

"You get one hundred thousand?" Fargo said. "Are you sure that's enough?"

"Yes, it will do quite nicely, thank you, for me to live out the rest of my life in luxury." Garson gazed wistfully westward. "The best clothes money can buy. Dining at the best restaurants. A fine carriage and horses."

"You have it all worked out."

"Down to the smallest detail," Tuck Garson said. "About four months ago I heard about the plan to push the telegraph through. I learned how important it was to the government. And I set myself to come up with a foolproof means of exploiting it to my advantage."

Fargo had been listening closely for evidence of a Southern accent and found none. "You're not from Kentucky," he flatly stated.

"Kentucky?" Garson said, then laughed. "Oh! You're referring to the stories told about me by those who don't have the slightest idea what they're talking about. Barroom gossip. Hearsay. Helped along by myself and my associates."

"Helped along?"

"Who do you think started that whole business about me being a highwayman from Kentucky? Whenever I've stopped at a saloon or a trading post, I'd make it a point to bring up Tuck Garson. Then I would confide in everyone present that I knew a friend who knew a friend who had heard from a second cousin the truth about Garson, and feed them some bull." Garson chuckled. "The stories they tell about me are marvelous. The jackasses spout drivel as if it's gospel."

"You did it so no one would ever suspect the truth," Fargo observed. As much as he loathed the butcher, he had to admit that Angus Stark had been right. Tuck Garson *was* a shrewd bastard.

"Ah, if you only knew the lengths I have gone to."

"Where are you from, then?" Fargo inquired. Simultaneously, he lowered his hands into the spring, the water rising up past his wrists, past the rope that bound them.

The mastermind wagged a finger. "That would be telling. I prefer that my past remain a secret. But I will share a few tidbits to convince you I'm in earnest. You must believe I will do what I say I will do, and you must make the commander of Fort Laramie believe you, too."

"Believe what?"

"More on that in due course." Garson idly rubbed his shin. "Where should I begin? How about when I was eight and killed both my parents? Slit their throats while they slept because I was tired of always having to do chores and being taken to the woodshed when I refused. I told the sheriff a man had broke into our house in the middle of the night, and he bought it."

Dallas was listening across the spring. "Your own parents?" he said. "You never told us that."

"Why should I? And what difference does it make?" Garson resumed his tale. "I went to live with an uncle. When I was fourteen I killed him and his wife, took the money they kept hidden in a flour bin, and went off to see the world. Got a job on a whaling ship. Glorious work, that was," he said fondly.

"You were a whaler?" Angus said.

Garson nodded. "For three years I slaughtered and butchered the biggest creatures on the planet. I loved cutting them up. All that blood, all those body parts. It was the only work I've ever truly enjoyed."

Fargo offered no comment when the older man paused. He was thinking that for all Garson's cleverness, the man wasn't in his right mind. Garson's next revelation left no doubt whatsoever.

"The blood was the best part of my work. God, whales have a lot! Many a time I would be hip deep in it. The feel, the fragrance—it was wonderful." Garson looked at his hands. "I've had a fondness for blood ever since I killed my parents. I remember dipping my fingers in theirs. I remember how sticky it was, how cool to the touch, how sweet it smelled."

Fargo wasn't the only one appalled. Dallas and even Stark were staring at their leader in undisguised worry.

Garson shook himself. "Anyway, when I was done whaling, I went to live in New York City. For a year or so I lived a perfectly normal life. Then my craving for blood got the better of me. I started cutting up derelicts and drunks and prostitutes. Not often, mind you. Maybe once a month or so."

"Is that all?" Fargo said, but it failed to get a rise out of Garson.

"As luck would have it, an off-duty policeman spotted me cutting up a dove one night and took me by surprise. Hit me with his stick. I was sentenced to twenty-five years in prison and after serving my full sentence, I got out about two years ago."

"And headed west?" the buffalo hunter said.

"Not right away, no," Garson said. "First I hunted down the policeman who had arrested me. I snuck into his home in the dead of night and killed him and his wife and their two daughters, and their dog. *Then* I headed west."

Fargo's disgust reached new heights. "After all that time you still wanted revenge?"

For the first time a crack showed in Garson's kindly exterior. His smile was replaced by a snarl and he rasped, "What a stupid question. The man deprived me of twenty-five years of my life! Of course I wanted him dead. All I thought about all those years was one day smearing my fingers with his fresh blood and laughing in his dead face."

Stark cackled. "You're a man after my own heart, boss."

Dallas, Fargo observed, was trying hard not to let his revulsion show, yet failing miserably. The Texan tore his gaze away and pretended to be interested in the horse string.

"My mistake was not going west right after my whaling days," Garson mentioned. "Out here I can indulge my passion to my heart's content."

"How many people have you killed since your release?" Fargo asked.

"I haven't counted them. Why that would be morbid, sir." Once again Garson was the model of friendliness.

Fargo twisted his wrists. Not much, but just enough to test whether the rope was soaked yet. To keep the madman talking, he commented, "Something doesn't add up. What does a man like you want with fancy clothes and carriages?"

"Well, I'm getting on in years," Garson said. "I'm tired of always sleeping on the ground and spending long hours in the saddle."

"All the money in the world won't keep you from the gallows if you go back to doing what you did in New York City."

"My urges do pose a problem, I'll admit," Garson said. "But I'm not as cocky as I was in my youth. I think things out more. If I'm careful, I imagine I can go on indulging myself until I keel over from old age."

Fargo moved his wrists back and forth as much as the rope allowed, which wasn't much. It would take some doing to loosen it enough.

"Over the past year I have met other men a lot like myself," Garson said, encompassing those around them with a sweep of an arm. "Men who harbor no love for the law. Men who like to kill as much as I do."

Angus Stark slapped his thigh and guffawed. "No one likes it as much as you do, Mr. Garson."

"Not quite, Mr. Stark. There have been others. I read about a woman once, a countess over in Hungary, I believe it was, who liked to bathe in blood."

The buffalo hunter was astounded. "She liked to take baths? Didn't she know they're bad for the health?"

"You're missing the point. The countess killed young girls and drained their blood, then bathed in it. She believed it kept her beautiful. By her own admission, she murdered more than six hundred peasant girls before the authorities arrested her. *Six hundred!*" Garson repeated almost reverently. "What a woman she must have been! I would very much have liked to have made her acquaintance."

"It's probably a good thing you didn't, boss," Stark said. "There wouldn't be any of those Hungary folks left."

Tuck Garson burst into peals of unchecked mirth, holding his sides and rocking from side to side as if fit to bust.

Fargo seized the opportunity to strain against the rope again.

"Angus, you are a joy to have around," Garson told his underling. "I will miss you when we come to the parting of our ways."

"Why part at all?" the buffalo hunter said. "I wouldn't mind visiting a big city and taking in the sights."

"We've been all through that," Garson said. "After we divide up the money, we must scatter to the four winds. Every military post from Canada to Mexico will be put on alert, and every lawman from here to Hades will be after the reward. We have better odds of eluding them if we go our separate ways than if we stick together."

Fargo thought of something. "You say that you've had this planned for four months?"

"Oh, much longer. Ever since I got out of prison I've

been on the lookout for a way to acquire a lot of money, and then I learned abut the telegraph. It was a godsend, you might say." Garson sat up. "Thanks to the false stories I've spread about myself, when I go into hiding the law won't have any idea who they're after. I'll be the next best thing to invisible."

Fargo recalled Major Canby complaining how Garson could ride right into Fort Laramie and no one would know. As loco as the madman's scheme was, if by some miracle Garson pulled it off, he could go anywhere he pleased with no fear of being caught. "What if they don't pay? All the trouble you've gone to will be for nothing."

"They'll pay," Garson said confidently. "There's no doubt of that, not with the part *you're* going to play."

"I'll die before I help you," Fargo said bluntly.

"I believe you. But I never said you would be a willing participant. Be thankful I have any use for you at all. If I didn't, I would have slit your throat by now." Rising, Garson picked up the Spencer. "Dallas, I'd like for you to keep an eye on our friend here. I need to talk with the Baxter brothers."

"Will do," Dallas said.

Tuck Garson and the buffalo hunter ambled toward the fire, and Fargo seized the opportunity to work his wrists back and forth. "Doesn't it bother you, riding with a lunatic?" he asked to distract the Texan.

"Shut up."

"Or what? You'll shoot me? Garson wouldn't like that, and you saw what he does to those who cross him."

"Don't remind me," Dallas said sullenly.

"This is more than you bargained for, isn't it?" Fargo mentioned. "How did you tie up with a man like Garson, anyhow?"

"Valdez and I had to leave Texas in a hurry. The Rangers were after us, and once that outfit sets their sights on a man, they don't rest until they catch him." Dallas sighed. "It was my fault. I got into a scrape over a woman. The daughter of a rich rancher. Her brother objected. He didn't think I was good enough for her.

One night he caught us together, one thing led to another, and he smacked me."

"So you shot him," Fargo said. Texans were notorious for not allowing others to lay a hand on them. Slap a Texan and the offended party would slap leather.

"I didn't shoot to kill, only to wing him. But he did a border shift. So I had to put two slugs into his chest."

The border shift, as Fargo knew, was a feat only experienced gun handlers dared attempt. When wounded in one arm, they would flip their revolver into the other hand, catching, cocking, and firing it in one smooth motion.

"The girl started screaming," Dallas recollected. "She was holding her brother and crying and telling me how she never wanted to set eyes on me again. Soon after, a warrant was out for my arrest, and the Rangers got on my trail. So I lit a shuck." He gazed in the direction Honta had dragged the *pistolero*. "Poor Valdez tagged along. We'd known each other since we were kids, and—" The gun shark suddenly stopped. "I talk too damn much sometimes."

"It's not too late to make amends," Fargo said. "Ride to Fort Laramie. Look up a Major Canby. Tell him I sent you. Tell him the truth about Garson and lead his troops back here."

"Nice try."

"You're really going to let Garson get away with killing your pard? I thought Texans were loyal to the bone."

Dallas glared at him and dropped his hand on the butt of his ivory-handled Smith and Wesson. "Damn you. Even if I wanted to, I couldn't turn on Tuck. The others think too highly of him. They wouldn't rest until they made me pay."

"Provided they live," Fargo said.

"Some are bound to. And I don't want to spend the rest of my life looking over my shoulder." Dallas pointed at the buffalo hunter. "Stark, there, can drop a buffalo— or a man—at five hundred yards with that buffalo gun of his. Honta is part Apache, they say. And that hombre with the goatee, Billy Sutton, is wanted in four states. Not to mention the Baxter brothers."

Fargo nodded. "I understand. You're scared to buck them."

Flushing scarlet, Dallas started to jerk the Smith and Wesson. "If you weren't tied up, I'd turn you into a sieve. I'm not afraid of any man. But I'm not dumb, either. I'm not about to commit suicide just to help you. And that's exactly what I'd be doing."

"Problems, gentlemen?"

Fargo wanted to kick himself. Unnoticed by either of them, Tuck Garson had returned and was regarding them with amusement.

"No problems," Dallas said quickly. "We just had a little disagreement. I wouldn't really shoot him."

"I hope not, for all our sakes," the terror of the plains responded. "The part he's to play is crucial." Garson focused on Fargo. "I can see a warning is in order. Behave yourself from here on out. It's in your own best interests. That is, if you want to get out of this alive."

"I wouldn't mind," Fargo said.

"Then use your head and keep a tight rein on that tongue of yours," Tuck Garson directed. "Don't try to turn my own men against me."

Since it would be useless to deny the accusation, Fargo said, "You can't blame a man for trying. You would do the same thing if you were in my place."

"Perhaps I would," Garson said, "but I'm not in your boots, and that's what counts." To the tall Texan he said, "Why don't you go give the Baxter boys a hand and send Billy over here?"

Billy Sutton was in his early twenties, with hawkish features and dark beads for eyes. On his right hip was a Remington, worn butt forward. On his left hung a Bowie. "What can I do for you, Mr. Garson?"

"You're to watch our friend here. He's not to say a word to you. Not one word. If he does, use that pig-sticker of yours and cut off a toe for each word he says."

"Whatever you want," Sutton said eagerly, drawing the big knife.

Tuck Garson winked at Fargo. "A word to the wise. I want you alive, but you don't necessarily need to be in one piece." And at that, he laughed and sauntered off.

9

Skye Fargo spent all afternoon loosening the rope enough to move his wrists. Whenever no one was looking he strained against his bonds and slid his arms back and forth. He couldn't exert all his strength or someone was bound to notice. But he was able to loosen it enough that when the time came to make a bid for freedom, it would be that much easier.

The day dragged by. The outlaws ignored him. When Honta returned, Tuck Garson sent the half blood right back out again. It wasn't until shortly before twilight that Honta returned a second time.

By then the Baxter brothers had the deer's haunch roasting over the fire, and the other cutthroats had gathered around to await their portion.

Garson looked toward the spring. Beckoning, he called out, "Billy! Bring our guest over here!"

Sutton was all too glad to comply. Ever since it became apparent that Fargo wasn't going to give him an excuse to chop off a few toes, the young hardcase had been restless and bored. He'd thrown stones into the air, drawn circles in the dust, sharpened his Bowie, spit on his boots and rubbed them clean. At one point he had turned to Fargo and declared, "Say something, will you? Just one word." When Fargo refused, Sutton sighed and went back to chucking small stones. "I hate it when we sit around doing nothing," he grumbled. "I just hate it."

Now, jumping up, Sutton grabbed Fargo by the arm and roughly shoved him toward the others. "You heard the boss. After you."

Tuck Garson patted a spot beside him. "Right here will do, Mr. Fargo. I thought you might like to know how you fit into my little plan to become filthy rich. We can discuss it over supper."

Fargo sat facing the butcher. He saw Dallas across the fire, sitting apart from the rest. To the left was Honta. The half-breed had squatted with his arms across his knees and was watching in peculiar fascination as blood dripped from the meat.

"Before we get to that, though, there is something I must know," Garson said. "Who were the two Indians you were with?"

Taken by surprise, Fargo blurted, "Indians?"

Garson's hand whipped up and around and caught Fargo across the face. The sharp *slap* was like the crack of a whip. All eyes turned. His expression as maddeningly serene and pleasant as ever, Garson said, "Just as I won't abide stupidity in others, I won't tolerate having my own intelligence insulted. Honta backtracked you. He found where you parted company with two men wearing moccasins and the tracks of several horses, only one of which was shod. He says the men were Sioux, although how that can be puzzles me. The Sioux aren't exactly the friendliest redskins alive."

Fargo's cheek stung. He tasted the salty tang of blood in his mouth, seeping from his split lower lip, and spat out the blood. "He's right. They are Sioux. A while back you butchered their loved ones and they're after your hair."

Garson was unfazed. "You don't say? It must have been those girls we caught picking berries. They were Sioux, as I recall."

"I remember them, boss," Angus Stark declared. "Sweet little things they were. Some put up quite a tussle. Which was fine by me. I like it when a gal fights and scratches. More fun that way."

"I cut one girl's eyes out," Garson mentioned. "It was disappointing, though. There wasn't as much blood as I thought there would be."

In all Fargo's travels he had never met anyone as un-speakably vile as the grinning monster in front of him. "If you're really as smart as you think you are, you'll head for parts unknown before the Sioux get their hands on you."

"Run from a couple of lice-ridden savages? I think not. We have enough hardware to hold off a small army." Garson made a tepee of his fingers and rested his chin on them. "So you hooked up with two warriors who are bitter enemies of all whites, is that what you're claiming?"

"We had an agreement," Fargo said.

"Did you? Or maybe that's just what they wanted you to believe. Honta told me they rode off to the northeast, taking your horse." Garson snickered. "Five will get you ten you'll never see the heathens or your animal ever again. They played you for a fool."

Fargo couldn't deny it was possible. The Sioux were renowned horse thieves. But he refused to believe Ante-lope Horn had deceived him. The warrior had been too sincere. The pair had ridden off to avoid being caught or killed, was all.

One of the Baxter brothers was poking the haunch with a knife. "It's about done, Mr. Garson," he an-nounced. "Do you want me to start passing some out?"

"Go right ahead. And bring an extra slice over for our guest. It wouldn't do to starve him to death." Gar-son sank onto an elbow. "Now then, to what interests you the most. Your part in our little drama. You, sir, are to be the messenger. The bearer of bad tidings, if you will."

"To the army?"

"You catch on quick. Yes, to the commandant at Fort Laramie. He's far more likely to take the word of a famous scout like yourself than he would be to take that of a telegraph employee. When you tell him you've seen us kill Western Union workers with your own eyes, when you inform him we're holding some as hostages, he'll take it as gospel. The military and the government will know we mean business."

"Don't do it," Fargo said.

"Don't what? Send the message? Or kill a few workers to prove I'm in earnest? In all great enterprises there is a cost."

"They're just doing their jobs."

Tuck Garson nodded. "That they are. But it's their misfortune to be in the wrong place at the wrong time." Plucking a blade of grass, he stuck the stem between his lips. "Tomorrow my men and I are going on a hunt. A human hunt. And you'll be a witness."

Fargo wasn't a bloodthirsty man. He tried to avoid violence wherever possible, tried to avoid shedding blood unless it was absolutely necessary. But at that moment he would gladly smash Garson's head to a gory pulp, and enjoy doing it.

"Have a care, sir. Your eyes betray you. I am not above putting one of them out if you offend me. You'll still have another to track with."

Gazing into the distance to hide his roiling emotions, Fargo made a silent vow. If it was the last thing he ever did, he was going to plant Tuck Garson six feet under. Or, better yet, leave Garson's torn and battered body lying on the prairie for the scavengers to dispose of.

The outlaws were in fine fettle. They joked and laughed during the meal, then stayed up until near midnight swapping stories. Not Dallas, however, Fargo noticed. The morose Texan kept to himself and only spoke when spoken to.

Fargo couldn't wait for the cutthroats to turn in. He was anxious to escape. His Arkansas toothpick was nestled in its sheath in his right boot, and once everyone was asleep, he would cut the rope, swipe a horse, and ride hell-bent for leather to Fort Laramie. With his assistance, Major Canby would run down the outlaws in no time, putting an end to Tuck Garson's blood-soaked spree.

Then Garson rose. "Time to turn in. We need to get

an early start, and it will be a busy day." He turned to Billy Sutton. "Mr. Fargo needs to be tucked in good and proper. The chore is yours."

The young gunman was all too happy to oblige, and scooted toward a saddle.

Fargo didn't like the sound of it. When Sutton rushed back bearing a length of rope, he coiled to run. The sight of Honta with a leveled rifle rooted him in place. Sutton pushed him onto his back and tied his legs.

"There. That should do it, boss."

"Check his wrists," Garson directed. "He had all afternoon to work on them."

"But I was watching him the whole time," Billy said.

"Were you, indeed? Even when you were tossing rocks and doodling in the dirt? What a marvel you are, to have eyes in the back of your head!"

Sutton grabbed Fargo's arms and gave them a yank. His brow puckering, he bent low and moved Fargo's wrists from side to side as much as the rope permitted. "I'll be! It is a bit loose."

"Redo the knots," Garson said. "And add another piece of rope as insurance." He smiled at Fargo. "I hope you won't hold this against me."

"Go to hell."

Tuck Garson laughed in wicked glee. "I probably would if there were such a place. But hell and heaven don't exist. They were concocted to keep people like you in line by those who are too weak-willed to take what they want when they want it."

Once Billy Sutton was done, Garson tested the ropes himself. "You did good, boy," he complimented the gunny.

Sutton puffed out his chest. "If you ever want anything, you only have to say the word, Mr. Garson. Thanks to you, we'll all be rolling in money before too long."

"Such devotion is touching," the butcher said dryly, then smirked at Fargo. "As for you, I'll sleep a lot easier knowing you'll be here in the morning when I wake up."

Fargo was tempted to tear into the man, his arms tied or no, but he held his temper in check.

"Yes, sir," Tuck Garson said to no one in particular. "Tomorrow it starts. Months and months of painstaking planning will be put to the test. We're about to do what no one else has ever done, boys. We're going to lock horns with the U.S. government. And by the time we're done, the plains will run red with blood."

Shortly after sunrise the outlaws were in the saddle and heading south. Fargo was astride Valdez's mount, being led by the reins by Billy Sutton. The Baxter brothers were close behind, as watchful as hawks.

Garson gave Fort Laramie a wide berth, swinging to the west and then south again. He set Honta and the big buffalo hunter on ahead. Late in the afternoon the pair trotted up, Stark flapping his arms in excitement.

"There are dozens of 'em, boss!" he declared. "Strung out for mile after mile. All we have to do is take our pick."

"Did you see any troopers?"

"A small column riding east," Angus said. "I figure they're under orders to move up and down the line. But they can't be everywhere at once."

Garson scratched his chin. "We'll bide our time. Lay low another night, then move in tomorrow when we're sure the boys in blue are nowhere around. It wouldn't do to be reckless with so much at stake."

They made a cold camp in a dry wash. Fargo again had to endure having his legs tied, and spent most of the night unable to sleep, racking his brain for a way of turning the tables on his captors. He kept hoping Antelope Horn and High Bull would show. Their prolonged absence did not bode well.

At first light Garson sent Honta out yet again. Along about the middle of the morning the half-breed was back, and after the two huddled, the order was given to mount up. Sutton and Dallas boosted Fargo into the saddle. Fargo glanced at the Texan but Dallas wouldn't meet his gaze.

For an hour and a half they rode to the southwest across gently rolling prairie. Coming to a rise, Garson called a halt, had everyone dismount, and climbed to the top with Honta and Stark. They weren't gone long. When they came back down, Garson was like a racehorse chomping at the bit.

"This is it, boys! Five wagons and eleven telegraph workers are half a mile away, putting up poles and stringing wire. We'll sit tight until they stop for the night, then pay them a visit."

"How many will we use as hostages?" one of the Baxter brothers asked.

"I haven't decided yet," Garson answered. "It depends on how good a mood I'm in. No more than two or three, though."

Fargo's gut churned. All those innocent men about to be slaughtered and there was nothing he could do! Or was there? Sidling over to where Dallas stood, he said quietly, "Are you really going to let them go through with it?"

"I'm just one man," the Texan said.

"You can alert the soldiers—"

"We've been all through that," Dallas interrupted testily. "Quit trying to appeal to a conscience I don't have."

"You're not like the rest of this bunch. You're not a bad man at heart."

"Whether I am or not isn't important. I agreed to ride with Garson, and I'm a man of my word."

Fargo refused to give up. "Did you know what he was like when you agreed? Or did you find out later when you saw him carve people up as if they were slabs of beef? Were you there when those Sioux girls were killed?"

Dallas's mouth was a thin slit.

"Did you see him cut out that girl's eyes? Did she scream? Beg for mercy? How did you feel afterward?"

The Texas was about to reply but just then someone snorted like a mad bull and shadows fell across them.

Tuck Garson, Angus Stark, and Honta were a couple of yards away, Garson with his hands on his hips and glaring at Fargo. "Maybe I should gag you until we're done. How would that be?" His eyes darted to Dallas. "Why did you let him prattle on? He's trying to turn you against your brothers in arms."

"Is that what we all are?" Dallas said.

For only the second time since Fargo had met him, Tuck Garson lost his smile. Garson took a half step, then glanced at the Texan's waist, at the ivory-handled Smith and Wesson. Dallas's hand hung next to it. "Assuredly, my friend," Garson said suavely. "We share a common bond. We're all desperados, all wanted somewhere or other for sundry crimes. We owe it to ourselves to stick together."

"Until we get the money and split it up, at any rate," Dallas said without enthusiasm.

"Exactly. Then you can take your share and go wherever your heart desires. Start a whole new life if that's what you want."

A chortle from the buffalo hunter ended the tension. "New life, hell! I'm going to spend mine on whiskey and women! I'll get drunk and stay drunk for a year! And have a different gal each and every night."

"We all have our dreams," Garson addressed the Texan. "By cooperating, we can each help the other's come true. Is that too much to ask?"

"No," Dallas said.

Fargo's hope withered, and he despaired of being able to save the workers. It was frustrating beyond measure. So much so, that when the buffalo hunter laid a brawny hand on him and pushed, an inner dam burst. Seething, Fargo pivoted and slammed his leg against Stark's. The big hunter tumbled, landing flat on his back. Suddenly leaping high into the air, Fargo bent at the knees and brought them smashing down onto Stark's stomach. The big man howled.

Springing off, Fargo cocked his boot to kick Stark in the head but a jarring blow between his shoulder blades pitched him onto his face. His injured side speared with torment. Twisting, he braced himself to rise but changed his mind when a rifle muzzle was jammed against his cheek.

Holding it was Honta.

"Don't kill him!" Tuck Garson commanded. "We need him, remember?" Marching over, he seized Fargo by the collar and jerked him upright. "You just won't learn, will you?"

Angus had sat up and was pressing his arms to his gut. Livid, spittle frothing his lower lip, he snarled, "Let me carve on him some, boss! A couple of fingers is all I ask! Or maybe rip out his tongue!"

"How will he tell the commander at the fort about our hostages if he can't talk?" Garson responded. "But the finger idea has merit."

"I knew an hombre once who had a finger chopped off," Dallas interjected. "Just one measly finger. But he wouldn't stop bleeding. They tried and tried but nothing worked, and he bled to death."

"That's not possible," the buffalo hunter declared.

"I recall hearing about a condition once," Garson said. "I can't remember the name the doctors gave it, but whoever has it can't stop bleeding."

"Do you want to take the chance?" Dallas said, nodding at Fargo. "Lose your messenger and the army might not take the message so seriously."

Garson's eyes narrowed. "How gullible do you think I am? The condition is rare. If Fargo has it, I'm the queen of England. Still . . ." He appraised Fargo. "You get to keep your fingers for the time being."

Angus Stark swore. "It's not right, boss. No man stomps on me and lives to brag about it."

"Look him up after this is over," Garson suggested. "Settle accounts then."

"See if I don't!" Angus said.

* * *

The killers sprawled out in the grass, some dozing, some checking weapons, others crowing about how they would spend their share of the money.

Fargo was entrusted to Billy Sutton once again. He sat with his legs bent so his boots were within quick reach but he was unable to palm the toothpick without being caught. In growing dread, he marked the westward arc of the sun.

A change came over the outlaws when the sun began to dip below the horizon. An air of excitement gripped them. They talked in whispers, and when a horse stepped on a rock and it gave a loud *crack,* half of them jumped, their hands falling to their hardware.

Soon a sliver of moon and a multitude of stars ruled the heavens.

Tuck Garson instructed everyone to mount up. "Mr. Stark, I want you to take Dallas, Clell and Keel around to the south. When you see us ride in from the north, you do the same. No gunplay until I say so." Garson lifted his reins. "Oh. Before I forget. Billy, you and Crane are to keep an eye on Mr. Fargo. If he so much as lets out a peep, pistol-whip him senseless."

The band separated, the two groups riding on around the rise rather than go up over it and risk silhouetting themselves against the sky. A shimmering patch of light in the distance was their destination.

Fargo intended to warn the Western Union crew, come what may. He didn't care what happened to him. Saving lives was worth the sacrifice. But when they drew within earshot, Billy Sutton drew a revolver, thumbed back the hammer, and pressed the weapon against his bruised ribs.

"I don't care what the boss says, mister," the gunny whispered. "You're not costing me ten grand. Make a sound and I'll do a hell of a lot more than pistol-whip you. I'll send you to meet your Maker."

Tuck Garson was well in front of his underlings, his rifle in its scabbard. He approached the circle of five wagons with his hands out from his sides so the workers could plainly see he was unarmed. "Hail the camp!"

Forms near the fire rose. Only a few held rifles. A voice that was all too familiar acknowledged the hail.

"Howdy there, stranger! Who are you and what's your business?" George Melton hollered.

Fargo recognized Charlie and others. Next to a van were two figures in baggy clothes and floppy hats. Icy claws sheared into him, and even though he had a gun to his side, he opened his mouth to yell.

"Do you reckon I'm bluffing?" Sutton warned, jabbing the barrel of his gun hard into Fargo's aching side again. "If so, you'd best reckon again. For ten thousand dollars I'd kill my own kin."

Garson rose in the stirrups. "We're out of Fort Laramie! Scouts sent to look for the Garson gang. Mind if we come in and light a spell? Your coffee sure smells inviting."

"Be our guest," Melton said merrily. "We can always use the company."

Garson kneed his animal into a gap between two of the wagons, then halted. With his friendly smile and demeanor, he must have seemed as harmless as a minister to the unsuspecting workmen.

Sutton and the others hung back at the fringe of darkness so that no one would get a good look at them.

"We're grateful for the invite," Garson said, stalling to give Angus Stark and company time to get into position.

Melton introduced himself. "I'm in charge of this crew. We've been stringing wire since sunrise and we're beat." He paused. "You say that you're after that Garson fella? The one who goes around whittling on folks like they were chunks of wood?"

"The very same," Garson said.

"I hope you get the scum," Melton said. "Alive or dead doesn't much matter, just so he and the vermin who ride with him don't go around murdering people anymore."

"Strong words."

"Not strong enough," the unwitting Melton rejoined. "Haven't you heard about all the evil things he's done?"

"I can recite every gory little detail," Garson said. "But I wouldn't call him and his men scum."

"What would you call them, then?"

Out of the night to the south materialized the big buffalo hunter and the rest of Garson's bunch. At the sound of the hoofbeats, Melton and the telegraph crew glanced toward the newcomers in confusion.

"What's this? More of you?" Melton said. "How many are there?"

"Enough to get the job done," Tuck Garson answered.

The telegraph crew were clustered by the fire, easy targets. Carrie and Carina, who hadn't moved from near their van, were partly in shadow. Fargo hoped the cutthroats would overlook them, but no such luck.

The Texan was angling in their direction.

At a wave from Garson, the outlaws moved past the wagons and spaced themselves around the increasingly worried workers.

"What's this?" Melton nervously inquired. He spotted Angus Stark. "Wait! I've seen that man before. He's no scout."

"A glimmer of intelligence," Garson said. "I'm impressed. Keep going."

"If he's not a scout, neither are you," Melton said.

"You're on a roll, friend."

"Why did you lie to us? What do you hope to gain?"

"Two hundred thousand dollars," Garson said, yanking his rifle from the scabbard. On cue, the other hardcases flourished their own rifles and revolvers.

George Melton was slow, but he wasn't dimwitted. "You're Tuck Garson's men!" he exclaimed, and thrust a finger at Angus Stark. "And you must be Tuck Garson himself! I suspected as much all along!"

Fargo wasn't the only one who had leaped to the wrong conclusion. The buffalo hunter erupted with mirth, while the real Tuck Garson walked his mount up close to the flustered supervisor.

"You were doing so well there, too. But you have it all wrong, pilgrim. I'm the man everyone is after. I'm the scum you mentioned." Growling like a feral beast, Garson struck Melton over the head with the stock of his rifle, and Melton crumpled. "I'm the one who is about to bleed you like a stuck pig."

10

Skye Fargo had seldom felt so helpless. People he knew, men who had never done anyone harm in their entire lives, were about to be horribly butchered by a living example of all that was foul and perverse in human nature. And there was nothing he could do about it.

Compounding the situation were the two women. At any moment Garson or a henchman might discover the brothers were really sisters. Carrie and Carina would be raped, and worse. Already Dallas was over by their van, his Smith and Wesson out, covering them.

The sight of harmless old George Melton, on his hands and knees with blood oozing from a nasty gash in his temple, was more than Fargo could abide. He didn't care if Billy Sutton shot him. He didn't care if Sutton and Crane pistol-whipped him. He couldn't sit there and do nothing while Tuck Garson gave free rein to his sadistic impulses.

Abruptly slapping his legs against the horse, Fargo moved into the light and snapped at Garson, "Let them be!"

It was hard to say who was more surprised, Garson or the telegraph crew.

Charlie gaped and exclaimed, "Mr. Fargo? Is that you?"

Another wailed, "Oh, Lordy! They've caught the Trailsman! What chance do the rest of us have?"

George Melton, rising unsteadily, a hand pressed to his head, said, "Fargo? Have they hurt you any?"

And from over by the van where the sisters stood

came a piercing, "Skye!" Carina had forgotten herself, and started to rush toward him. Fortunately, Carrie had the presence of mind to grab her.

Fargo thought for sure the outlaws would realize her cry had been that of a woman, but they didn't seem to notice. They were glued to the man they had hooked their stars to, with good reason.

Gone was every trace of Tuck Garson's kindly facade. In its place was a mask of fury fit only for nightmares. Garson was glancing from Fargo to the telegraph crew and back again as if he couldn't decide who to kill first. "Billy!" he suddenly roared.

Sutton rode forward, blatantly scared, "Yes sir, Mr. Garson, sir? What do you need done? You name it, I'll do it."

Garson thrust a finger at Fargo. "I told you to keep an eye on him! I told you if he let out a peep to knock him senseless!"

"He took me off guard, sir," Sutton said. "But it will never happen again. I'll collect him and take him off a ways so he won't bother you none. If you want, that is."

Fargo had to act quickly. He glanced toward the sisters and was surprised to see the Texan had leaned down and was whispering to them. Hoping they would either flee or dive under the van when the shooting commenced, he shifted toward Melton and said in a rush, "George! Listen to me! These men are going to kill you and most of your crew. There's no reasoning with them. No talking them out of it. Do you understand? You must fight for your lives! You must fight them *now*!"

"Shut up, damn you!" Tuck Garson bellowed. Turning his mount toward Fargo, he elevated his rifle to do as he had done to Melton.

"Boss! Look out!" Billy Sutton cried, and his six-gun spat flame and lead.

A telegraph worker, who had aimed a gun at Garson's back, dropped in his tracks.

The next moment all hell broke loose.

Some of Melton's men opened fire, others charged the

cutthroats, still others attempted to run. In retaliation, the outlaws banged away wildly, some of their mounts plunging and rearing and whinnying.

Shots boomed and thundered. Men screamed, cursed and railed. Bedlam ruled the night. Hardcases and Western Union employees were in a frenzied battle for their lives, filling the camp with clouds of gunsmoke and the shrieks of the dying.

In the midst of the melee, Fargo tried to turn his horse toward the Darrwoods, but the animal was petrified by the din and balked. Sliding off, Fargo rotated toward their van only to find his path barred by a milling mix of men and mounts.

Somewhere Tuck Garson was hollering over and over, "Don't kill them all! Don't kill them all!"

A rearing bay pranced toward Fargo and he danced aside to avoid its flailing hooves. Stray slugs whizzed by and clods of dirt were kicked up as he zigzagged toward the van. Then, in front of him, he saw one of Melton's men and the gunny called Crane grappling on the ground.

Fargo's wrists were bound but he still had the use of his legs. Taking another step, he slammed a boot against Crane's check, dazing him, permitting the worker to gain the upper hand. The man tore Crane's pistol from his hand, shoved the muzzle against the gunman's torso, and triggered two shots.

Fargo didn't linger. The Western Union people were giving a good account of themselves but the outcome was inevitable. They were outnumbered and outgunned. He spied Charlie thrashing about and stopped to render aid. Suddenly another sound ripped the night. A woman's scream.

Hunching over, Fargo veered toward the sound. He thought he spotted a figure in a floppy hat struggling against two hardcases but he lost sight of them in the cyclone of pandemonium.

A second later an unforeseen development added to the rampant confusion. Melton's crew had tethered their horses inside the circled wagons, as Fargo had advised them. Now, spooked by all the shooting and shouting, they broke loose. Horses barreled every which way, and it was all Fargo could do to keep from being bowled over or trampled. The gunmen and the telegraph crew were in the same predicament. Fargo witnessed a panicked buttermilk plow into Billy Sutton's animal and they both went down, Sutton cursing a mean streak.

Pausing, Fargo scanned the camp. Between the horses and the raging clash and the spreading gunsmoke, he had little chance of finding Carrie and Carina and being able to spirit them to safety. Especially trussed up and unarmed. Garson would soon take him captive again. He had to get out of there, had to shed the rope and arm himself. Then, and only then, could he be of any help to anyone. It galled him, though, turning and sprinting toward the wall of darkness with the women unaccounted for. He kept telling himself it was for the best.

Unexpectedly, a rider hove out of the acrid smoke. Fargo dug in his heels and slid to a stop. Looking up, he beheld the leering visage of the lanky gun shark called Clell. The man had a Starr revolver pointed at his head.

"Where in hell do you think you're going, mister?"

Fargo went to dart past the gunman's mount but Clell expertly kneed it forward, thwarting him.

"Stand still, damn you, or I'll put a bullet into your knee."

Just then two shots blasted near at hand, two incredibly swift shots that stiffened Clell's spine as if it were an ironing board. The lanky killer swiveled and tried to level the Starr but a third shot bored a hole squarely between his eyes and he pitched backward.

Out of nowhere came another rider. It was Dallas, his reins in one hand and the smoking Smith and Wesson in the other. "Stand still! I'll grab hold!" he shouted. Bending low, he hooked his arm.

Bewildered but not about to decline, Fargo felt the Texan lift him bodily into the air. Dallas's spurs flashed, and the horses sprang into a gap between the wagons and trotted off across the prairie. "There are two women!" Fargo yelled.

"I know! Valdez saw through their disguise that night we paid you a visit." Dallas reined to the left.

Fargo glanced back. The scene was one of rampant confusion, the uproar loud enough to be heard for miles.

Twenty yards out, Dallas suddenly drew rein and let go. "I'll help you climb on the other horse!" he barked.

What other horse? Fargo wondered, and pivoted. Behind him, mounted bareback on a dun, was a short figure in baggy clothes. In the dark he couldn't see the figure's face clearly enough to tell who it was. "Carrie?" he guessed.

"No. Carina," the younger Darrwood responded. "I think those polecats got their mangy mitts on my sister."

Dallas leaped down and grabbed Fargo by the shoulders. "I'll throw you up in back of her. The two of you can ride double."

"First look in my right boot," Fargo directed.

"Your boot?" Squatting, Dallas did so. "Tricky cuss, aren't you?" he said, palming the Arkansas toothpick.

"Get this damn rope off!" Fargo goaded. He was sick to death of being tied, of being hampered. When the Texan complied, he flexed his fingers and rubbed his wrists, restoring the circulation.

A rifle thundered deep in the swirl of smoky combat, the retort louder than all the rest, the unmistakable blast of the big buffalo Sharps favored by Angus Stark. Fargo looked for sign of Carrie Darrwood, but trying to distinguish one person from another in the frantic whirl of antagonists and animals was hopeless.

"Get on!" Dallas urged.

"We can't leave Carrie!" Carina protested. "We have to go back for her!"

Dallas was striding to his sorrel. "We do, and not one of us will make it back out alive! We can do her more good by sticking close and waiting our chance."

"Skye?" Carina pleaded. "Please! She's my sister!"

Fargo wavered. The Texan's suggestion was the wise thing to do, but he was reluctant to leave Carrie in the madman's clutches. A whoop from the camp decided the issue for him. It was the buffalo hunter.

"We've won, boys! We've won!"

Out of the smoke growled Tuck Garson's voice. "Check and see how many are still alive! Honta, find Fargo! Angus, bring that one you've caught over here!"

"Carrie!" Carina said, and made as if to gallop toward the wagons.

Instantly, Fargo snagged her bridle, then the reins, and swung up behind her. "Now isn't the time."

Carina tried to jostle him off. "Let go! What kind of man are you? We can't desert her!"

"We're not going to," Fargo said, and brought the animal around. Holding to a walk so as not to be heard by the outlaws, he rode to the south, circling to where he could see the center of the camp. Then he halted.

Dallas had followed. "We should move further off," he recommended. "They're liable to spot us if we're not careful."

"I need to hear what they say," Fargo said. "But you can take Carina if you want."

"Like hell," the hothead snapped. "I'm not leaving until I know how my sister is. She could be hurt."

The smoke was slowly dissipating. Vague shapes moved about. Men coughed and muttered. Others groaned in agony. One man was blubbering like a baby with the colic.

"I wish I had a gun," Fargo remarked softly. If they were spotted, he wanted a fighting chance.

"Thanks for reminding me," Dallas whispered, and twisting at the waist, he opened a saddlebag. "Garson gave this to Billy Sutton, but I took it from the kid's bedroll earlier today when he was off heeding nature's call." He produced Fargo's Colt. "Sorry I couldn't get your Henry. Honta has taken a shine to it and carries it with him all the time."

"I'm grateful," Fargo said, checking to verify cartridges were in the cylinder. "I owe you. And you owe me an explanation."

"Later," the Texan promised.

"Look!" Carina declared louder than she should, and pointed. "Isn't that Tuck Garson yonder?"

That it was, near the fire, holding his Spencer and standing over one of over a dozen bodies that dotted the camp. The Baxter brothers were on either side of him, rifles to their shoulders. Honta was roving about, examining the fallen. Billy Sutton was reloading his revolver.

Approaching Garson were Angus Stark and Keel. They had hold of Carrie. Her hat had fallen off and she was struggling mightily but she was powerless in their grip. When they came to a stop, the buffalo hunter shook her violently and rasped, "That's enough! Behave or I'll slug you."

"Only one of the crew is alive?" Tuck Garson said. "That's all?" He stomped a foot like a riled bull. "Damn it all! We need more hostages if we're to persuade the army to give in to our demands. One man just isn't enough."

"How about one *woman*?" Angus said.

"A female?" Garson gazed around the battleground. "Where? She would be worth her weight in gold."

"Right here." Angus nodded at Carrie. "Under all these baggy clothes is a gal. See for yourself."

Tuck Garson did just that. He placed his right hand on the older sister's chest, and his eyes widened to the size of walnuts. "I'll be damned!"

"Take your filthy paw off me!" Carrie fumed. Lashing out with her foot, she connected with Garson's shin. He winced, then brutally backhanded her across the face so hard, she sagged in her captors' grasp.

"That will be enough out of you, girl." Garson grasped her by the chin and jerked her head from side to side, inspecting her as if she were a horse he planned to purchase. "This is most peculiar. Since when does Western Union hire females?"

"Who cares, boss?" Angus said. "She's what we need, ain't she?"

"That she is, Mr. Stark," Garson said, his grin restored. "That she most definitely is! In fact, having her is better than having a dozen male hostages. The army will never endanger a woman. They'll fall over themselves to do as we want until she's safe and sound."

Billy Sutton finished loading and twirled his pistol. "Then this didn't turn out so bad after all, did it?"

"Clell and Crane are dead, and we can ill afford to lose them," Garson said. "But once again things have turned out better than I dared hope. I—"

Honta jogged over, the Henry in his left hand. "Fargo not here," he reported in thickly accented English.

"He slipped away during the ruckus?" Garson stared off into the darkness to the east. "The coward. I should have known all the tales they tell about him aren't true. No one can be that tough."

"Dallas gone also," Honta revealed.

"Both of them?" Angus said. "Do you reckon they were in cahoots, boss? They sure were talkin' together a lot."

Garson swore. "I never did trust that Texan. He was too squeamish about carving people up." He looked at the breed. "Anything else?"

"Two workers live. One gone."

"Gone how? Dead?"

"Missing," Honta clarified. "I count when we come. Not same now."

"So one of them got away, too?" Garson pursed his lips. "I don't like it, boys. Don't like it one bit. Fargo, Dallas, or the Western Union lackey could be hightailing it to Fort Laramie right this second. Or going to alert the other Western Union crews."

Angus wrapped an arm around Carrie's waist. "We should light a shuck, then, while we still can."

"First things first," Tuck Garson said, and placed a hand on the half blood's shoulder. "Show me the two who are still alive."

Fargo watched as the outlaws walked to a middle-aged man who was curled up in a ball and moaning pitiably.

"Hell, this one won't last the night," Garson grumped. "Where's the other one?"

The second man was Charlie. The scarecrow had a bullet wound in his thigh and another in his right shoulder. He cried out when Garson ordered Billy Sutton and Keel to drag him over to a wagon and prop him against a wheel.

Garson hunkered and gripped the front of Charlie's shirt. "I want you to listen to me. I want you to listen good."

"Y-y-yes sir," Charlie stammered.

"This is your lucky night. You get to live. We'll leave you water and jerky. Some of your fellow workers or a cavalry patrol will be along eventually. You're to tell them what happened. You're to let them know I've taken the woman as a hostage."

"What woman?" Charlie asked.

Garson snapped his fingers. Angus brought Carrie over and pushed her onto her knees. "This one," Garson said.

Befuddled by pain, Charlie squinted. "You must be plumb loco, mister. That there is Darr, one of two brothers on our crew. He's not no woman."

"Isn't he?" Garson retorted. His arm streaked out like a striking rattler. Before Carrie could think to stop him, he had grabbed the top of her shirt and wrenched, popping buttons and exposing her chest. "Then how do you explain these?"

Carrie covered herself, but Charlie had seen enough to astound him.

"Darr? You're a girl? Does that mean your brother is a girl, too?"

"There's another female?" Garson shot to his feet and scanned the bodies. "Honta? Was she killed in the gunfight?"

"No. The rest all men. I check."

"Damn!" Garson spat. "What I wouldn't give to get

my hands on her. Two women hostages would be even better." He leaned toward Charlie. "When help arrives, tell them about Darr, here." He nodded at Carrie. "Tell them I'll kill her unless they meet my demands. Assure them I will cut her into bits and pieces and send the pieces to the fort as keepsakes if the government doesn't pay us the two hundred thousand. Can you remember all that?"

Fargo saw Charlie nod. He also felt Carina's hand slide over his to grip the reins. "Don't even think it," he whispered.

"We have to get her out of there!"

"Quiet down!" Fargo shushed her. "When the time is right we will. We would never get close enough now."

"He's right, ma'am," Dallas whispered. "There are seven of them, and only Fargo and me. They'd drop us before we reached her."

Their words were wasted. "We have to do something!" Carina said. Elbowing Fargo in the ribs, she tugged on the reins, but Fargo held on. Their horse moved to the left, confused by the conflicting signals.

"Enough!" Fargo whispered, clamping a hand over Carina's mouth and yanking her back against him. "You'll get your sister killed if you don't calm down."

Over in the circle of firelight, the outlaws were reclaiming their mounts. A mare was brought for Carrie, and she was shoved up onto it, but not allowed to touch the reins. Angus held on to them.

Billy Sutton carried a water skin and saddlebag to Charlie. "Here's your grub and water, mister."

"Hurry it up, boys," Tuck Garson ordered. "Help could arrive at any time." He looked down at the wounded workman. "Can I count on you not to forget my message?"

"I won't forget," Charlie said. "Not with that girl's life at stake. Just don't hurt her. She's never done anything to you."

"Whether she lives or not depends on whether I get

my money," Garson said. "Make that abundantly clear to everyone."

Charlie glanced at Carrie. "I'm awful sorry, missy. But don't worry none. The soldiers won't let any harm come to you."

Carrie said something Fargo didn't quite catch. Then Garson bawled for the gunmen to head out and the entire bunch filed off to the northwest.

"Do you have any idea where they're headed?" Fargo asked Dallas.

"Garson has a spot staked out off in the hills," the Texan disclosed. "The roost, he calls it. He took us all there once to show us. He aims to lie low until the month is out, then send a rider to Fort Laramie for the money."

"Can you find it again?" Fargo asked. It would simplify matters. Otherwise, they had to trail the cutthroats, a difficult task at night.

"I reckon I can."

Fargo rode toward the firelight. "We'll leave you with Charlie," he told Carina. "Look after him until someone comes."

"I'll do no such thing," she snapped. "When you rescue Carrie, I want to be there. You're taking me with you."

"Can't you listen for once?" Fargo avoided a wagon tongue and reined up almost on top of the wounded worker, who about jumped out of his skin.

"Mr. Fargo! You scared me half to death! Who is that with you? Wood?"

Fargo climbed down and sank onto a knee. "We heard everything, Charlie. We're going after Garson. Can you hold out until help shows?"

Charlie was pasty and sweaty, his shirt and pants stained with blood. "Don't worry about me. Darr is more important. She was so scared. I could see it in her eyes." He looked up at Carina. "Are you a girl, too, Wood?"

"Afraid so, Charlie."

"Imagine that. All those nights sleeping on the prairie, me dreaming of pretty girls, and the two of you were close enough to touch. Don't that beat all?"

Fargo opened Charlie's shirt. The bullet had gone clean through, and the bleeding had stopped. The same with his leg, he discovered. "You'll be feverish and weak for a while but it will pass. Drink a lot of water." Fargo slid the lone water skin left by the outlaws within easy reach. "Are there any more of these around?"

Carina answered. "In the supply wagon. I'll fetch one."

"Fetch two," Fargo said. It was enough to last a week, and should more than suffice. "And bring extra food!"

Charlie smiled thinly. "I haven't felt this puny since that summer I was bit by a cottonmouth. Darned near killed me."

"If I could, I'd stay with you," Fargo said.

"Do what you have to." Charlie gazed at the bullet-riddled bodies and tears filled his eyes. "I'm the lucky one. Did you see what they did to George? Shot him again and again and again, like they were shooting a rabid dog. Even after he was down, that gunny with the goatee pumped more slugs into him." Choked with emotion, Charlie paused. "George was my friend."

"They'll pay," Fargo vowed.

"See that they do."

A sudden clatter of hooves brought Fargo around in a crouch with the Colt extended, but it was a riderless horse with a saddle, the one that belonged to Clell. It had bolted when Dallas blasted its owner into eternity.

Slowly going over so as not to scare it, Fargo seized the bridle. He returned to Charlie just as Carina set down two more water skins and a large pouch crammed with bread and other food.

"This should do me," Charlie said. "Now you'd best fan the wind after them fellas."

Carina was already climbing on the animal she had shared with Fargo. "You heard the man. Let's go! I want to stick close to Carrie in case she needs us."

The hothead and the Texan trotted off.

"Help will come," Fargo told Charlie, hoping to high heaven he was right. Then he clucked to his mount and hastened into the night.

11

The hills were high and rugged, their slopes ungodly steep. Lower down they were heavily timbered and rife with deadfalls. Above the tree line they were strewn with treacherous talus. The outlaw roost, Skye Fargo learned from Dallas, was on the highest hill to the west. It gave the cutthroats a commanding view of the entire countryside.

Tuck Garson had chosen wisely. A cavalry patrol couldn't get anywhere near the hideaway without being spotted. The deadfalls and talus were bound to slow them down, giving Garson and his killers ample time to slip away.

But Fargo was counting on three people being able to do what thirty could not.

They had ridden all night to get there. Hugging thick timber, Fargo wound steadily deeper into the hills until the roost was in sight. Then he moved into a stand of firs and dismounted, announcing, "This is as far as we go. We'll rest here until sunset."

Carina, true to form, objected. "And leave my sister alone with those brutes all day long? Where are your brains? Dribbling down your leg? Think of what they'll do to her!"

"They won't lay a finger on her," Fargo said. "Garson needs her alive and untouched, at least until he gets the money."

"You don't know that for sure," Carina argued. "They might see fit to have their way with Carrie anyway."

"Whatever else he might be, Garson isn't stupid,"

Fargo said. "The army will insist on sending an officer to prove she is unharmed before they hand over the money. Garson won't dare let his men touch her until then."

Dallas had slid down and was stretching. "He's right, ma'am. I know Tuck better than most. He wants to be rich more than anything in the world, and he won't let anyone spoil his plans."

"Maybe he won't let his gunnies near her, but what about Garson himself?" Carina asked bitterly.

"Garson doesn't have any interest in that sort of thing," the Texan responded. "Sex, I mean. His idea of fun is to carve a woman up like he did those Indian girls. That's what he'll—" Catching himself, Dallas said, "I mean, that is, don't fret just yet. Your sister will be fine for the time being."

Carina folded her arms, closed her eyes, and said sorrowfully, "I can't believe this is happening. I just can't. If anything happens to her . . ." She couldn't go on. Tears trickled, and she bowed her head.

Fargo draped an arm across her shoulders. Quietly sobbing, Carina leaned against his chest. He let her cry herself out, and when she was done, he guided her to a clear spot and gently lowered her to the ground. "Rest a while."

"I suppose I should. I'm tuckered out."

With the Texan's help, Fargo stripped the horses and picketed them. He spread a blanket over Carina to keep her warm.

Dallas spread out his bedroll, plopped onto his back, and pulled down his hat brim. "I reckon I'll catch up on my shut-eye, too. You should do the same. Tonight won't be a turkey shoot."

"I will in a while," Fargo said. Hiking westward, he came to a spot where he could see the outlaw stronghold. He studied the terrain leading up to it, memorizing landmarks and plotting how best to reach the summit without being detected. Preoccupied, he didn't realize someone had come up behind him until he heard a footfall a few feet to his rear. He spun, his hand dropping to the Colt.

"It's just me," Carina said. "I didn't mean to spook you."

"I thought you were sleeping."

"I tried and tried but all I did was toss and turn. I'm too worried about Carrie." Carina gaze off up at the high hill. "So that's where they've taken her? It'll take us hours to get there."

"We should reach it about midnight," Fargo said. By then most of the gun sharks should be asleep. If all went well, he could slip in and whisk Carrie out of there without firing a bullet.

"I guess she and I should have known something like this would happen," Carina said. "What were we thinking? Two women pretending to be men. On the frontier, no less! We had heard about all the dangers. We just never took them seriously."

"Too few do," Fargo said.

"No one ever thinks that bad things will happen to them. It's always supposed to happen to the other fella."

"That's not how life works."

"We could be back in Ohio right now working as seamstresses. Earning a pittance, sure, but back there a woman can go where she pleases in safety. No one is out to cut her to pieces." Tears flowed again, and Carina mewed like a kitten. "I should never have let Carrie talk me into it."

"Stop being so hard on yourself," Fargo said, taking her into his arms. His shoulder bumped her hat and it fell off. Caressing her short hair to comfort her, he said, "There's a saying that hindsight is always best. But you had everyone hoodwinked until Tuck Garson came along. If not for him, you would have pulled it off."

Carina wrapped her arms around his waist and pressed her face to his buckskin shirt. "You're a peach, Skye Fargo," she sniffled.

Fargo had been called a lot of things, but he couldn't recall ever being called that before. Tired, he stifled a yawn, then felt a stirring in his groin. The warmth of her body and the feel of her warm breath on his chest was arousing him. He tried to shift so it wouldn't be obvious, but Carina gave a little start, then glanced up wearing a mischievous grin.

"Is that a pistol in your pants or are you thinking about the other day in the van?"

Fargo smiled and shrugged. "Let's get you back so you can rest."

"What's your rush?" Carina responded, and rising onto her toes, she kissed him hotly on the mouth, the tip of her tongue darting out and rimming his lips. When she pulled back, she brazenly placed her hand on the bulge in his pants. "Mmmm. Nope, it's not a pistol. And it's bigger than it was a minute ago."

"Are you sure about this?"

"Why not? It will help me take my mind off Carrie. And I'll be able to doze off afterward." Carina lightly rubbed his redwood, hardening it even more. "What do you say? Care to do a girl a favor?"

Only an idiot would refuse, Fargo reflected. They were safe enough for the time being. The Texan was too far off to hear, and the carpet of pine needles underfoot would be as soft as a bed. Besides, he wasn't ready to turn in just yet, himself.

"If you decline I'll be crushed," Carina said impishly. "A woman likes to think her charms are equal to any occasion. Are mine?"

In answer, Fargo slid his hands down over her back, cupped her firm posterior, and ground his still growing bulge against her. His mouth covered hers.

Carina groaned lustily when he slid a hand between her legs and stroked her. "Oh, my!" she declared when their kiss ended. Her cheeks were flushed, and she was breathing as if she had jogged a mile. "The things you do to me! You make me tingle clear down to my toes."

"I'm just getting started," Fargo said and kissed her once more, letting it linger on and on as their tongues swirled and glided and his hands roamed up across her flat stomach to her breasts. He squeezed them, eliciting the loudest groan yet, and she sagged against him, her hands reaching out to remove his buckskin. When the shirt was off she gasped at the purple-yellow bruise running down his side.

"Poor baby, you're hurt," she said tenderly.

"Not so bad that I can't treat a woman," Fargo replied. He took her breast into his mouth as she started moaning again.

"You're like delicious wine," Carina said huskily. "One sip is never enough. I've been dreaming of you ever since the last time."

"Dreaming what, exactly?" Fargo teased.

"About doing this, for one thing," Carina said, and pried at his belt buckle. She placed his gun belt on the ground, then parted his pants, exposing him to the world. Licking her lips, she sank onto her knees.

At the contact of her wet lips, it was Fargo who groaned. His hands on either side of her head, he relished the sensations she provoked. When he couldn't stand it any longer, when he was on the verge of exploding, he sank onto his own knees. Their mouths joined, and he peeled at her clothes, removing her shirt, shoes and britches. Gently, he eased her onto the pine needles.

Carina lay with one knee bent, her hips swaying seductively, her mouth a delightful oval as ripe as lush fruit. Her nipples were hard, her breasts inviting. Through hooded, sultry eyes, she regarded him and playfully said, "What are you waiting for? An engraved invite?"

Fargo removed his boots and pants. He placed the toothpick next to his Colt, both inches from his right shoulder. Then he parted her legs and stooped forward, his tongue diving into her core.

Carina arched her back and panted, her nails digging into his shoulders. "Ohhhh. Yesssssss."

Fargo licked and sucked. Her thighs clamped to his ears, and she heaved upward each time his tongue brushed her swollen knob. When his tongue was sore and his chin was matted with her delicious juices, he rose onto his knees and aligned his member at the entrance to her sopping wet tunnel.

"Do me," Carina said. "Do me hard and fast."

Out of habit, Fargo quickly scanned the woods, insuring they were alone. Once or twice over the years he had been caught with his pants down, and it was not an experience he would recommend.

"Please," Carina pleaded, misunderstanding his delay. "You can't change your mind *now*."

"Not now, not in a million years," Fargo said, and abruptly thrust up into her, sheathing himself to the hilt.

"Ah! Ah! Oh, mercy!" Carina's pert bottom rose up off the ground, her eyes wide, her mouth wider. "I'm—I'm—"

She was gushing already. Fargo felt her inner walls contract and ripple, and it was all he could do not to do the same. He rocked his hips, nearly lifting her rear into the air as she clung to him, lavishing his neck and chest with fiery kisses.

"Yes! Yes! More! More!"

Fargo placed his mouth on her right breast. Inhaling the nipple, he tweaked it with his tongue and pinched it with his lips. Carina's hips drove against him in abandon, and she bit him on the shoulder.

Holding her close, Fargo suddenly rolled onto his back, carrying Carina with him so that they wound up with him on the bottom and her on top. A lecherous smile animated her as Carina placed her hands on his chest.

"I get to ride you for a while, is that it, handsome? Suits me just fine. I like being in the saddle as much as I like being ridden."

Fargo explored her satiny body as Carina rocked on him as if he were a hobbyhorse. Her head tossed back, she wheezed like a chimney sweep, her breasts jiggling with each downward motion of her velvet thighs. She gasped. She whined. And before too long she exploded in another paroxysm of passion that left her drained and limp, her forehead on his chin.

"I could do this forever," Carina breathed.

Fargo stroked her back, running a finger down her spine. He massaged her inner thighs, her stomach, her mound. For her part, she nibbled on his arm, licked his neck, and sucked on an earlobe.

Clasping her tight, Fargo rolled back over, ending up on his knees. Carina's arms rose to his shoulders. With her nipples jutting skyward, her face aglow with carnal craving, and her body so soft and yielding, she was exquisite.

Carina must have been thinking the same about him because she cooed huskily, "The woman who finally corrals you is going to be damned lucky."

"You think so?" Fargo said, and smothered her mouth with his lips while spearing up into her. She matched his ardor, the two of them moving rhythmically. Her hands were all over him; his neck, his chest, his hips, his legs.

The forest around them blurred as Fargo drifted in a sea of pure pleasure. He pumped and pumped, and when Carina cried out and her inner walls wrapped tight around him, he exploded. For long minutes afterwards, they rocked together as one. Eventually, spent and panting, they coasted to a stop.

Drowsy, Fargo cushioned his cheek on her left breast and closed his eyes. The rising and falling of her chest lulled him to the border of dreamland.

Carina ran a hand through his hair, then traced his ear with a forefinger. "A person could get used to that."

"You don't say?" Fargo sleepily replied. Rousing himself, he rolled off her and onto his back. They lay quietly for a while. Just when he was about to fall asleep again, Carina nudged his arm.

"Promise me something."

"About us?" Fargo had hoped she wasn't the kind to make demands.

"No, about Tuck Garson."

"It depends on what the promise is," Fargo hedged.

Only a fool gave his word without knowing what was required.

"Promise me that if Garson has hurt Carrie, you'll hurt him, and hurt him bad. Carve on him just as he's carved on others. Cut off his fingers, his ears. Make him suffer just as his victims have suffered."

"I plan to kill Garson whether he's hurt your sister or not. A man like him can't be allowed to roam free. But I won't do it the way you want. I won't torture him."

Carina turned on her side so she faced Fargo. "Why not? Think of how many people he's brutalized. It's the least he deserves."

"Quite a few would agree with you. But if I slice him up before he dies, I'm no better than he is."

"You refuse to stoop to his level? Is that what you're telling me? Ordinarily, I'd say that's damn decent of you. But this is Tuck Garson we're talking about. An inhuman ogre. If it were me, I'd gut him and make him eat his own innards. Or chop off his fingers so all he has are stumps."

Fargo cracked an eye. "You're a bloodthirsty little minx."

"Can you blame me? You knew George Melton. You saw how sweet and friendly he was. A nicer man was never born, yet look at what Garson did to him. Garson is evil, through and through."

Not feeling inclined to debate her, Fargo tried to drift off to sleep but Carina was too overwrought to let him.

"If there's any justice in this world, any justice at all, Tuck Garson will die as horribly as all his victims. Isn't that only fair?"

When Fargo didn't respond, Carina nudged him again. "Isn't it?"

"Only fair," Fargo mumbled.

"I just don't understand this world of ours," Carina said. "My ma dying when Carrie and I were little. My pa falling and breaking his neck. Sweet Mr. Melton lying back there on the prairie in a pool of his own blood."

Sighing, Fargo sat up. "What don't you understand?"

"Why the Almighty lets horrible things happen. Why we're put on this earth just to suffer and die. It doesn't hardly seem right to me. What do you think?"

"I think—" Fargo began, and stiffened when the breeze bore with it a low whinny. Shoving up off the pine needles, he heard another whinny, only it wasn't uttered by the same horse. "Get dressed," he instructed her, grabbing his pants.

"What's wrong?"

"Maybe nothing," Fargo said. By right, the horses should be dozing. They were exhausted from their all-night ride. But something had disturbed their rest.

Carina was putting her clothes on as fast as she could. "Do you think it's Garson? Or some of his killers?"

"Anything is possible," Fargo said. It could just as well be hostiles or a grizzly on the prowl. "Hurry."

"You can go on ahead if you want," Carina said. "I'll catch up."

Fargo wasn't about to leave her there. Not when she was unarmed. Hurriedly donning his clothes, he waited for her to get done. As she wedged her hat onto her head, he grabbed her wrist and glided eastward, weaving among the boles, his right hand on his Colt.

Everything seemed to be just fine.

Dallas was stretched out right where they had left him, the brim of his hat still down over his eyes. The three horses were still picketed, their heads drooping, none showing sign of alarm.

"I guess we were worried over nothing," Carina commented.

Fargo was set to agree. Then he saw a *fourth* horse, saddled, off in the shadows, its reins dangling. "Someone else is here," he warned her, and started to slide the Colt from its holster.

"I wouldn't do that, were I you." Two metallic clicks sounded, and from behind a tree stepped a swarthy man in a black hat and vest, a cocked Remington in each hand. His shirt was partway open, revealing wide bandages that crisscrossed his slim chest. Wedged under his gun belt was another pistol, Dallas's ivory-handled Smith and Wesson.

"Frank Brody," Fargo bit out. Releasing the Colt, he slowly hiked his arms. He wouldn't risk an exchange of lead with Carina at his side. She might take a slug meant for him.

"In the flesh," Brody said. "No thanks to you."

"Two bullets are enough for most."

"Another couple of inches closer to my heart and I wouldn't be standing here." Brody sidled to the left so he had a clearer shot. "Dallas, you can quit pretending you're asleep now."

The Texan pushed his hat back and frowned at Fargo. "He snuck up on me while I was asleep. Threatened to drill me if I warned you."

"I still might plug you," Brody declared spitefully.

"How did you find us?" Fargo asked.

"I wasn't hunting you, mister, if that's what you're thinking. I was on my way to the roost, and made camp about a mile back late last night. This morning the three of you woke me up when you rode by."

"Lucky us," Dallas said.

"I didn't know what to make of it," Brody said to Fargo. "You, that boy, and the Texican all together. But I saddled up and trailed you."

"What now?" Fargo took a step away from Carina.

"I'm taking you to see Tuck Garson," Brody responded. "You were heading that way anyway, so you should be right pleased at how considerate I'm being."

Dallas sat up. "That's what I was doing. Taking them to Garson. Give me back my revolver and we'll get going."

"The idea occurred to me," Brody said. "Then I got to wondering why this hombre"—he indicated Fargo—"was wearing his iron, and why the two of you were acting so chummy." Brody's weasel eyes narrowed. "No, I'm keeping your pistol. I don't rightly know what's going on here. We'll let Tuck get to the bottom of it."

Fargo took another slow step away from Carina while

commenting, "I can't wait to meet him. I want to join his gang."

"You?" Brody said skeptically.

"Why not?" Fargo said. "I hear a man can earn a lot of money riding for Garson."

Frank Brody glanced at Dallas. "Been flapping your gums, have you? So this is why you're taking him to the roost."

"I tried to tell you," the Texan said.

Brody pointed a revolver at Carina. "How does the boy fit in? I remember seeing him at Honest Jack's. He works for Western Union, as I recollect."

"Do you also remember Garson saying we needed hostages?" Dallas said.

The gun shark was perplexed, and it showed. Their lies were plausible enough to be true. "It could be as you say," he admitted. "We'll find out soon enough."

Again Fargo took a step. He was hoping for a distraction, for the chance to jump the killer, but Brody swivelled toward him.

"Make like a bump on a log, bastard, or I'll ventilate you six ways from Sunday." Brody jerked his chin toward Carina. "You there, boy. Saddle the horses and be quick about it. No tricks, hear?"

Nodding, Carina scurried toward the animals. In her haste, she moved as she normally would, her hips swaying from side to side.

Frank Brody noticed. "There's something mighty strange about that kid," he said, more to himself than to Fargo or the Texan. The next second he called out, "Hold it! Stop where you are!"

Carina obeyed.

"Turn around," Brody ordered. "Take off that godawful hat."

Casting a worried look at Fargo, Carina did as she'd been instructed. "What's gotten into you, mister?" she asked the gunman in her best imitation of a male.

Instead of responding, Frank Brody intently studied her face, her body. "It can't be!" he declared, again more to himself than anyone else. "Take off your shirt. I want to see what's underneath."

"I'll do no such thing," Carina said defiantly.

"I'll count to ten. If you haven't shed that shirt by then, your friend here takes lead." Brody pointed a revolver at Fargo's gut. "One. Two. Thr—"

"I'll do it!" Carina cried. In her anxiety, she used her normal voice. "Just don't shoot him!" She began undoing the buttons.

Fargo girded himself to leap. In two bounds he could reach Brody. All he needed was to wait for the right moment.

"Faster, damn you!" the gun shark snapped. "At the rate you're going, it'll take you until the middle of next week."

Carina was beet red, either from embarrassment or anger or a mix of both. "I wish I had a gun!" she exclaimed.

"Wishes are for whiners," Brody said, sneering. "My pa taught me that when I was knee-high to a calf, shortly before he left my ma for parts unknown. And I learned the lesson well. In this life a man has to take what he wants."

Six of the eight buttons were unfastened. Carina's shirt hung in loose folds, and she was holding her arms in such a way as to keep it from opening all the way.

Dallas began to rise but a flick of Brody's pistol stopped him. Sinking back down, he asked, "What do you hope to prove? Why make the boy do this?"

"Boy, hell!" Brody said. "If what I suspect is true, he's really a she. It makes me wonder about that so-called brother of his."

Fargo glanced at Carina. The moment of truth was almost upon them. She only had one button left to go. Then she would open her shirt. For a second or two Brody would only have eyes for her.

"You're making a mistake," Dallas tried one last time.

"Keep your worthless opinions to yourself," Brody said.

Carina was done. Glaring at the gunny, she hissed, "Is this what you wanted to see, you snake in the grass?" And she flung her shirt wide.

Instantly, Fargo leaped—only to find himself staring down the barrels of Frank Brody's nickel-plated Remingtons.

12

Skye Fargo was a dead man. He couldn't possibly reach
Frank Brody before the beady-eyed gunman fired, and
it was plain by Brody's expression he was going to do
just that. Fargo flung his arms out to try and knock the
Remingtons aside, when suddenly there was a whizzing
sound and the *thok* of flesh being transfixed.

Brody staggered backward, gaping at the feathered
end of a shaft that protruded from his chest.

Fargo stopped cold. He heard the whizzing sound
again, and a second arrow sheared into the weasel just
above the navel.

Howling in pain and outrage, Brody rotated toward
the forest. He took a halting half step, then collapsed,
oozing to the ground like so much sludge. His arms
twitched twice, and that was all.

"Injuns!" Carina breathed in terror.

Out of the woods came Antelope Horn and High Bull.
The former had another arrow nocked for use, but it
wasn't needed.

"Kill them before they kill us!" Carina declared much
louder, and with a fearful yell she sprang to Brody's
body. Prying a Remington from his hand, she pivoted
toward the warriors.

"No!" Fargo reached her before she could shoot and
grabbed her arm. "Don't! They're on our side."

"You know them?" Carina marveled.

Antelope Horn and High Bull had stopped and were
regarding her warily. "The white woman wants to shoot
us?" Antelope Horn said.

"She does not know you are a friend," Fargo said, and walked over. "I was beginning to think you had changed your minds."

"About counting coup on the killers?" Antelope Horn responded. "So long as there is breath in our bodies we will not give up."

"We followed you after you left us," High Bull detailed. "We saw them capture you. But there were too many for us to help."

"Where did you disappear to?" Fargo was curious to learn.

Antelope Horn answered. "We suspected they would backtrack you. It is what we would have done. So we took the horses and went off across the prairie. When night fell, I snuck back and waited for a chance to slip in to cut you free. But there was always someone watching you. And at night they took turns standing guard."

High Bull took up the account. "When they rode out we followed at a distance. Last night we heard shots and hurried to find out what the shooting was about. We saw wagons and many dead whites."

"We arrived just as you were leaving," Antelope Horn said. "We tried to catch up, but you were riding fast. Just before sunrise we stopped to rest our horses. And once it was light enough, we tracked you here." The young warrior glanced at Brody. "It is good we came when we did."

Fargo agreed. Thanking them, he reclaimed his Colt, then explained his pact with the two Oglalas to Dallas and Carina.

"Are you sure you can trust them?" the hothead wondered. She had swiftly buttoned her shirt and jammed her floppy hat back on her head. "I've heard all sorts of tales about the horrible atrocities the Sioux commit."

"Whites commit atrocities too," Fargo said. "As for trusting them, I think they proved themselves just now, wouldn't you?"

Dallas rolled Brody over to get his ivory-handled Smith and Wesson. Spinning it a few times, he twirled it into his holster with a fancy flourish and grinned. "In Texas we having a saying. 'Love your enemies but keep your gun oiled.' I reckon I'll take your word for it that they're friendly, but I'm not about to turn my back on them."

Antelope Horn was looking from one to the other. "Are they talking about us, Never Loses the Trail?"

"Yes," Fargo confirmed. "Like you, they are enemies of the men who killed your sister, and they are glad to have your help."

High Bull gestured with his lance. "Where are the killers? Do we leave now to go after them?"

"Not until dark," Fargo said. He deemed it prudent not to tell the pair about the roost just yet. The Oglalas might take it into their heads to rush on ahead. Struck by a thought, he stared off into the trees. "Do you still have my stallion?"

"Of course," Antelope Horn said. "We have watched over him as if he were our own."

"Even though he gave us trouble," High Bull said. "He kept trying to run off, to go to you. He is a fine horse."

"There are none finer," Fargo said sincerely. The Ovaro had carried him over more miles than most ten mounts, and never once let him down. He would sooner part with an arm or leg than part with it.

"We will bring the horses," Antelope Horn said. "But first . . ." Handing his bow to High Bull, he drew his long knife and walked toward Brody.

"What's he fixing to do?" Carina bleated in dismay. "Not scalp him, I hope?"

"I'd rather he didn't," Dallas said. "Brody wasn't my friend, by any stretch. But no one deserves to lose their topknot."

To Fargo it made no difference. Various tribes indulged in the practice. A few went one step further and mutilated their enemies. It was part and parcel of frontier life, and he rarely gave it a second thought. Still, to keep a rift from developing, he quickly said, "I would take it as a great favor, Antelope Horn, if you would not do that."

The warrior had leaned down and was reaching for the gunman's head. "Why not?" he responded, then gazed at Carina and the Texan. "It bothers them? Very well, Never Loses the Trail. For you, and only for you."

Another hour elapsed before Fargo could turn in. After stripping the Ovaro and brushing some burrs out of its mane and tail, he sat down with the Oglalas at their request and detailed the attack on the wagons. Neither were pleased about having to wait until sunset, but they honored their promise to obey him.

Carina was as skittish around the Sioux as a colt around a pair of mountain lions. She draped a blanket over her shoulders and sat with it bundled about her body to further disguise her gender. She need not have bothered. The warriors already knew, as Fargo learned when Antelope Horn posed a question.

"Why is the white woman so strange? The others I have seen all wore dresses, as our women do. But this one wears pants like a man. The other white women were clean and wore pleasing scents. This one has dirt all over her face and smells like a goat."

Fargo was at a loss to explain. Among a warrior society like the Oglalas, the men hunted and went to war, the women were in charge of the lodge and all that pertained to it. Women did not try to be men. Were he to tell the warriors what Carina was doing, they would think she was crazy. So he fibbed. "She disguised herself so the killers would not rape her."

Antelope Horn's eyebrows arched. "She disguises herself well. Had I not seen her when her shirt was open, I would not have guessed the truth."

Fargo spent the rest of the morning and most of the afternoon sleeping. He needed his wits about him for the dangerous work ahead, so when he awoke shortly after five, he prepared coffee and downed four steaming cups while he watched the sun sink toward the horizon.

No one spoke much. Carina made it a point to stay well clear of the Oglalas, which amused them.

Dallas was rolling up his bedroll to leave, when out of the blue he said, "Tuck Garson is mine. Make that clear to your Indian friends."

"Whoever gets the chance brings him down," Fargo said. "You can't turn this into a personal grudge."

"The hell I can't! Garson shot my pard."

"And the Oglalas lost family. They have just as much right to vengeance as you do." More so, in Fargo's view.

"Then it's every hombre for himself," Dallas said. "They just better not get in my way."

"What about me?" Carina surprised Fargo by saying. "Surely you don't expect me to waltz up there unarmed? I need a weapon. A rifle or a pistol, it doesn't matter. I can use either." Carina stared meaningfully at Brody's gun belt, which lay beside Fargo.

"I'd rather you stay with the horses."

"Oh. I see. Leave the poor, helpless female behind so she doesn't get in the way?" Carina bristled. "Don't hold your breath! It's my sister those no-accounts took! Unless you bean me over the noggin with a rock, you can count me in. And I'll need a firearm."

Against Fargo's better judgement he handed her the gun belt. "Brody was skinny enough, so this should fit you. Just don't do anything foolish. We'll never save Carrie if we don't use our heads."

Carina yanked a Remington out and admired the nickel plating. "Speak for yourself. I'm not letting anyone or anything stop me from killing Tuck Garson."

As if he did not have enough to worry about! Fargo mused. Were it up to him, he would leave the hothead *and* the Texan behind, and only take the Oglalas.

"I can't handle two pistols at once," Carina mentioned, wriggling the gun belt. "Who wants the extra?"

"Not me," Dallas said, patting his Smith and Wesson. "I'll stick with this. No one but a lunkhead takes a six-shooter he's never used into a gunfight."

"True enough," Fargo said. When a man's life depended on hair-trigger speed and accuracy, it was the height of folly to rely on an untested weapon.

Scarlet and yellow bands painted the western sky when they climbed on their horses and rode toward the highest hill. Fargo assumed the lead, glad to be on the Ovaro again. They left the horse he had been riding and Brody's animal behind, hobbled so neither could stray off. "They're my gift to you," he informed the Oglalas shortly before smothering the fire and mounting. "When this is over, you are welcome to come back for them."

To the Sioux, a horse was the greatest gift one man could give another. "We thank you, Never Loses the Trail," Antelope Horn had said, genuinely touched. "But we have nothing to offer you in return."

"Your friendship is enough," Fargo replied.

They stuck to dense cover until the sky changed from slate-gray to pitch-black. It slowed them down but was a lot safer. From then on, the landmarks Fargo had memorized acted as signposts pointing them steadily higher and nearer their confrontation with the worst pack of murderers on the frontier.

In due course the vegetation thinned but the slopes steepened. Worse, most were covered by talus. As treacherous as ice, as deceptive as quicksand, it was the bane of every horseman. The loose gravel and dirt cascaded like water whenever it was stepped on.

But early that morning Fargo had noticed that a few slopes here and there were bare, and he had worked out in his head how to gain the summit with the least amount of risk. At a plodding pace they climbed for hours on end, and as he had predicted, they didn't come within rifle range of the crest until near midnight.

Reining up at the base of a rocky knob, Fargo slid from the saddle. He considered again asking Carina to stay behind but branded it hopeless. She would balk, and argue, and at this point they had to make as little noise as humanly possible.

"Stay behind me," Fargo whispered as, palming the Colt, he started up the slope. They were at the north end of the hill, where Garson was least likely to expect an attack. Aside from a few dwarf scrub trees and boulders, it was barren.

Welcome darkness shrouded them, darkness so deep it was like being at the bottom of a well. Almost to the top, Fargo was surprised to hear the murmur of low voices. He'd hoped the outlaws would be asleep, but from the sound of things most were wide awake. His left hand scraping the ground to balance himself, he inched to within an arm's length of the rim.

Someone laughed loudly. Someone else swore. Fargo sank onto his stomach and snaked the rest of the way. Removing his hat, he raised his head high enough to take stock of the situation.

The top of the hill was essentially flat and about forty yards across. A small fire blazed at the center, ringed by the gang. Fargo saw Tuck Garson add part of a dead branch from a large pile. Along the southern edge were big boulders and to the west grew a solitary thicket. The horses were between the fire and the thicket. They were hobbled, from the look of things, so running them off was not an option.

High grass grew at the north end. Fargo crawled up into it, parting the stems with care so they wouldn't rustle. He counted seven huddled shapes around the fire, exactly how many there should be, but he couldn't quite see them clearly enough to tell who was who.

Fargo searched for sign of Carrie Darrwood. Saddles and blankets were strewn about close to the fire, and Fargo thought he saw a figure that might be Carrie lying among them. Or it might be saddlebags and a bundled blanket. He needed to sneak closer to find out.

Glancing over his shoulder, Fargo saw Dallas to his right and Carina a little to his left. The Texan was moving quietly but Carina was causing the grass to jiggle and shake. Bending toward her, he whispered, "Don't make noise!"

The grass parted and her grimy face appeared. "I'm not no damn Apache!"

Fargo was sorry he had said anything. In her anxiety over her sister, Carina might give them all away. Advancing cautiously, he scrutinized the faces of those around the fire. Tuck Garson was there, of course, smiling and talking. Angus Stark, the big buffalo hunter, was chomping on jerky. Billy Sutton was cleaning his pistol with a cloth. The bearded Baxter brothers and the lanky gunman, Keel, were listening to Garson. That left the seventh person, who picked that moment to shift and gaze forlornly into the night.

Fargo froze in place. It was Carrie! But that meant one of the cutthroats was unaccounted for, one of the deadliest of the entire bunch—Honta. Raising on his elbows, he scoured the roost.

At his left elbow the grass crackled. Carina had caught up, and she whispered impatiently, "What are you waiting for?"

"Be quiet," Fargo whispered. It was essential he find out where Honta had gotten to. The half blood could be anywhere.

"They can't hear me from here!" Carina said. "We've caught them flat-footed. Let's move in—"

Suddenly turning, Fargo grabbed her by the arm. "Quiet, damn it! One of them is missing!"

Carina would never learn. "So? He's got to be over there somewhere."

Fargo almost slugged her to shut her up. But just then, out of the corner of his right eye, he registered furtive movement. Instinct propelled him into shoving her aside and throwing himself to the right as the night spiked with flame and gunsmoke. Hot lead smacked into the earth where he had been lying. Twisting, he banged off two rapid shots, aiming at the rifle flashes.

Bellows and curses greeted the din as the killers leaped to their feet and fanned out. Tuck Garson seized Carrie and held her in front of him.

"Stay put!" Fargo instructed Carina. Rising into a crouch, he veered to the right, seeking to draw the half blood's attention away from her. Again a rifle spat flame, and lead buzzed by his ear. He answered, his two shots blending into one, then threw himself flat to reload.

More guns cracked and boomed. Some of the outlaws were moving toward the high grass, others were seeking cover.

A Sioux war whoop filled the air, then another. A bow string twanged. Twenty yards away, Keel tottered as if drunk, an arrow sticking from his sternum. Clutching it, he fell, triggering three wild shots into the soil.

Fargo was inserting new cartridges as fast as his finger could fly. He saw Tuck Garson haul Carrie toward the boulders. Angus Stark and Billy Sutton had wisely darted out of the circle of firelight, but not the Baxter brothers. They had acquired rifles and now commenced spraying the high grass.

Carina answered their volley and they focused on her. Fargo heard her yip, either from pain or fear. Shoving upright, he angled toward the horses, deliberately making a target of himself again to draw the Baxters' bullets. He succeeded all too well. Both men cut loose at him.

Fargo threw himself flat once more. He rose to shoot and saw one of the Baxters stagger and go down, an arrow through his thigh. The other brother rushed to help and dragged his wounded sibling out of the firelight.

At that, all the shooting stopped. The night was silent except for the nickering of spooked horses.

Fargo had lost track of Dallas and the Oglalas. Reversing direction, he snaked toward Carina. She had given her location away, and some of the cutthroats were bound to try and slink up on her. But when he reached the spot where she had been, she was gone.

On the one hand, Fargo was glad she had the foresight to change positions. But on the other, with Honta and the buffalo hunter lurking in the dark, she was in even worse peril. Bent grass showed him the direction in which she had gone. Wearily, he followed. He had gone five or six yards when a tremendous commotion broke out to the west, the fierce sounds of two men locked in mortal struggle.

Heavy breathing and the clang of steel, the earmarks of a knife fight, were momentarily drowned out by the thunder of a heavy-caliber rifle to the east. It was promptly answered by an equally loud retort only twenty or thirty feet from where Fargo lay. Angus Stark and High Bull, he deduced, engaged in a battle of buffalo guns, Sharps pitted against Sharps.

Fargo bore to the south, looking for Carina. The knife fight still raged, the constant peal of the blades testifying to the flurry of furious blows. Then there was a loud grunt, a thud, and a groan.

Six feet more, and Fargo stopped. Any farther and he would be bathed in the glow from the fire. Slanting to the right, he skirted the light and soon was near the horses. Rising and tucking at the waist, he took a step, then realized someone else had reared up a couple of yards away.

"I've got you, you polecat!" Billy Sutton declared, grinning wickedly. His revolver glinted dully.

"Try me, instead!" Out of nowhere, there was Dallas, his ivory-handled Smith and Wesson extended.

Billy spun and threw a shot. But in the time he fired once, the Texan fanned off three shots that slammed into Sutton and jarred him onto his boot heels. Billy teetered, gurgled, and crashed onto his back.

Dallas went to ground, giving Fargo no chance to thank him. Dashing past the string, Fargo ran to the south, seeking Garson and Carrie. On the right was the thicket. Directly ahead were the boulders.

Halting, Fargo strained for some sign of movement. Well to the rear boots pounded, and he whirled and spotted a pair of darkling figures. Rifles cracked, but the shots weren't aimed at him. The riflemen were firing into the high grass at Dallas, whose Smith and Wesson barked back.

The Texan had helped him. Now Fargo could repay the courtesy. "Baxters!" he shouted.

The bearded brothers turned. Fargo cored the one on the right and sent two slugs into the one on the left.

Both went down, but they were only wounded. Their rifles speared the darkness, angry lead buzzing Fargo as he continued to shoot. So did Dallas. Caught in a withering crossfire, the Baxters were soon riddled.

Dropping low, Fargo reloaded again, then stalked toward the pair to make sure they were dead. Their limbs and faces were contorted in the throes of violent death.

Fargo wondered why the Texan hadn't appeared. "Dallas?" he whispered. "Are you all right?"

"I took a slug but I'll live. Find Garson! We need to end it, once and for all."

Fargo's sentiments, exactly. Prowling southward, he passed the horses and was midway to the boulders when a gun hammer clicked. Spinning, he saw Tuck Garson with a revolver pressed to Carrie's head.

"Drop your gun or she dies."

Fargo's every impulse was to snap off a shot. Only six feet separated them. But in the dark, with Carrie so close to Garson, she might be hit. Galled at being caught flat-footed, he let go of the Colt.

"Excellent," Garson crowed. "I could have shot you down a moment ago, but then you wouldn't have known who did it."

"Does it matter?" Fargo said.

"It does to me. I can't tell you how much pleasure killing you will give me. You've been a thorn in my side since we met."

"I've tried my best."

Carrie tried to pull loose but Garson jerked her back and smacked the barrel against her temple. Wincing, she raised her bound hands to her head.

"Try that again and you'll regret it," Garson snarled. Then he thrust his pistol at Fargo. "The moment of reckoning is at hand. Any last words?"

Fargo would let his actions speak for him. He prepared to hurl himself forward, knowing full well he would never reach the madman alive. But fate dealt an unforeseen card in the form of Carina Darrwood, who materialized several paces from Tuck Garson, the Remington clasped in both her hands.

"I could ask you the same question! Drop your pistol and release my sister!"

Garson shifted just enough to see her. "Well, well. There's a fly in the ointment."

"I won't tell you again!" Carina said.

Fargo slowly tucked at the knees to retrieve his Colt. All he needed was one clear shot. Just one.

"Which did you say to do first?" Garson asked Carina. He was stalling, trying to rattle her, to confuse her, to gain an edge. "Release your sister? Very well." He shoved Carrie to one side. "There. Now I suppose you'll take me prisoner?"

"Wrong. Now I'll shoot you dead!" Carina declared, and stroked the Remington's trigger. Nothing happened. Frantic, she stroked it again and again, then blurted in horror, "I forgot to reload!"

"What a shame," Garson gloated, taking aim.

Fargo's fingers found the Colt. Instantly, he brought it up and fired. Garson stumbled, then swung toward him. They shot simultaneously, Garson missing by a whisker. Fargo was more accurate. He fired a third time as the butcher swayed like a reed in the wind, fired a fourth as Garson dipped onto his knees, and shot a fifth and final time as Tuck Garson flopped onto his face in the dirt.

Out of the darkness limped Dallas. "Is it over?"

"It's over," Fargo said.

But there was one thing left to do. They found Antelope Horn lying a few feet from Honta. Both bore multiple cuts and stab wounds; both were dying. Angus Stark was dead, his head blown half off by High Bull's Sharps. High Bull had taken a slug low in the stomach. He lingered another hour and died singing his death chant. His Sioux brother died minutes later.

Fargo buried the Oglalas so scavengers wouldn't ravage them. He was leaning on the shovel, weary to the bone, when Carina and Carrie came up on either side and looped their arms in his.

"We've been talking it over," Carina said, "and we'd like to thank you properly for all you've done."

"How about going off together for a few days, just the three of us?" Carrie suggested.

"How about for a week?" Fargo said, and they grinned.

LOOKING FORWARD!
**The following is the opening
section from the next novel in the exciting
Trailsman series from Signet:**

THE TRAILSMAN #229

MANITOBA MARAUDERS

*1861—in the northwest provinces of the giant
called Canada. A new land brings new
dangers unlike any faced before, where
sometimes the choice between compassion and
killing is no choice at all. . . .*

The big man riding the magnificent Ovaro let his lips
thin in a tight line. Habit was a terrible burden, he swore,
an unfair taskmaster, pushing you to do things you wanted
to ignore. It made today captive of yesterday. Regardless,
his lake-blue eyes stayed narrowed as he watched the
young woman nose her horse through a narrow passage-
way of jack pine and paper birch. He stayed in his own
nest of pine as his eyes shifted to the six horsemen that
followed her. They had split into two groups of three each,
one trio staying behind the young woman, the other in-

creasing speed to outflank her in the trees. Skye Fargo drew a deep breath and cursed habit again as he moved closer, cutting his own way through the thick woods.

This was not his land. He was a visitor here, a sightseer, a vacationer. He'd come wanting to see the land, to feel the majesty of it, and ride the beauty of it. He'd already seen how it had its own character, a magnificence at once awesomely beautiful and frightening. He had the feeling that here, in this vast land called Canada, beauty and richness existed as a temporary gift from the great fierceness of the northland. But trouble was trouble. It always had its own marks and wore its own signs. Skye Fargo knew those signs, and also knew that they were the same all over. They were why he sat in the pines and watched the six riders as they closed in on the young woman. Old habits refused to leave a man alone.

It had all begun in the little town of Lakeshore, in the small hotel near the west shore of Lake Winnipeg. Fargo had taken a room there, stabling the Ovaro and then sitting down to a drink of good Canadian whisky and a meal of jack pine savage venison roast. Six men were in a wooden booth just to one side of him, their voices carrying clearly. With a quick glance, he stole a fast look at them. All wore worn, raggedy outfits and all had the hard, tight faces of men who lived their lives scrounging at the bottom of the barrel. He'd seen their kind often enough back in the States.

"It's got to be her," a man with a red-and-black checked shirt said. He had a long nose and a pinched face that gave him a weasel-like appearance. "She fits the description," he continued. "They figured she'd be coming this way and looky here, she's all alone, boys."

"Then we do it," one of the others said in a gravelly voice. "If we make a mistake, so what?" he added callously.

Fargo looked away as he took another sip of his drink.

"We wait for her at the end of town?" one of the others asked.

"Two of us watch there come morning. Two of us stay here in case she's at the hotel. Two of us cover up and down main street," the one with the long nose said. "When we spot her, we follow her and find the right spot near the lake where we can dump her."

"Not before we have ourselves a taste of her," the gravelly-voiced one said.

"You got a one-track mind, Joey," the other snickered.

"You all want some too. I just say it," Joey's raspy voice answered. In agreement the group fell silent as they finished their meal. Fargo's venison roast came as they were leaving, and Fargo remembered telling himself it was none of his damned business. Here, he was a stranger in a strange land, determined to enjoy himself. He certainly hadn't come all the way up here to find trouble. Somebody else could see to it, he told himself and put it out of his mind as he attacked his venison. But by the time he finished his meal he was cursing old habits again. A young woman was going to die. He knew she would be beaten and violated by those animals, and then they would kill her. He'd never been able to turn his back on someone in trouble. He'd paid his bill and gone to his second-floor hotel room. A single bed and a dresser with a big pitcher of water waited for him there. It was all he needed he thought as he undressed, fitting his long frame onto the bed as best he could. He went to sleep knowing he didn't need to wrestle with making decisions. The past had already made them for him.

He'd set the inner alarm clock he'd learned to use and dressed before daybreak. He went to the stable, retrieved the Ovaro and wedged himself between two shacks that let him see the hotel. Two of the six men arrived and took up positions of their own, both near the hotel. The watching game had begun. Over an hour passed before the streets filled with wagons and riders.

Eventually, the girl came out of the hotel. Fargo glanced at one of the two men, saw him signal to the other and returned his eyes to the young woman. She wore a floppy, wide-brimmed hat that hid most of her face but he saw a well-formed figure, a brown vest over a tan shirt, Levis encasing slender legs, a neat, contained figure with what seemed to be modest breasts. She went around to the stable behind the hotel, finally emerging riding a dapple-grey gelding.

She rode down the main street, not hurrying, and the two men immediately fell in behind her, keeping their distance. Fargo moved from his vantage place, hung far back, and soon saw the first two men joined by the rest of the gang. The young woman rode away from town, staying along the wide road. Finally, she turned into the thick pine forests that spread out on both sides of the road. She rode up an incline that leveled off after about thirty yards. Fargo watched the men follow. He turned the Ovaro into a thick line of trees and moved closer as he saw the two groups of men speed up to close in on the young woman. She rode idly, pausing to admire flowers and trees, obviously simply enjoying herself. The riders split up into two groups, one set moved faster while the other trio hung back. Fargo kept pace with the first three and watched them surprise the young woman as they pushed out of the trees in front of her. Fargo took note that the long-nosed one led the troop.

"Heather Grandy?" the man asked.

"Who's asking?" the young woman said, her head lifting high enough to allow Fargo to see under the wide-brimmed, floppy hat. He took in a soft-lined face, quietly lovely, with wide, hazel eyes, full, red lips and a firm chin.

"You don't need to know that," the long-nosed one said.

"Then you don't need an answer," the girl returned.

"Don't be like that, honey. We came all this way to give you a good time," the man said, and one of the others snickered. As he watched, Fargo saw the young woman reach down and come up with a riding crop in her hand.

"Now what do you figure to do with that?" long-nose said chidingly. The young woman's arm snapped out with the speed of a lightning bolt, slashing the riding crop across the man's face. "Ow, Jesus!" he screamed as a line of red erupted on his face. He twisted in the saddle, lost his balance, and fell from his horse. The girl spun her dapple-grey and put the mount into an instant gallop racing away.

Her reaction had been so viciously swift that she might have made her escape. Unfortunately for her, she ran head-on into the second trio, which had come up behind her. With their guns drawn, they blocked her way and she reluctantly reined to a halt. "End of the road, honey," the gravel-voiced one said. "Drop it," he ordered, gesturing toward the riding crop. The young woman let the crop fall from her hand as the three men came forward, one taking hold of her mount's cheek strap. They led her back to where the long-nosed one still pressed a kerchief to his face. He rose from one knee and started for the girl.

"Kill her, goddammit," he snarled as the other three pulled the girl from her horse. He started to rush at her, but the others held him back.

"Easy, Bert," one said. "No sense in wasting a good thing."

"Bastards," the young woman spit out at her captors. She whirled around and tried to rake her nails across the face of the nearest man. He managed to twist away as one of the others slammed a fist into the girl's kidney from behind her. She gasped in pain and pitched forward onto her hands and knees. One of the others grabbed her arms and flipped her onto her back as a third one fell on top of her. He straddled her and began to tear her shirt open.

"Let's see what you got, honey." He laughed as the girl twisted helplessly. Fargo grimaced, the big Henry already out of its saddle case. He raised the rifle and fired. The one on top of her screamed in pain as the bullet shattered his shoulder blade. He fell off the girl and Fargo fired again. The one holding her arms flew backwards, both hands clutching at his abdomen. Fargo saw the other four, six-guns in hand, peering into the trees as they searched for their attackers. The girl had smartly rolled herself into a ball and lay still. Fargo slid silently from the saddle. He knew the four men would zero in on his voice, or his next shot. They'd send bullets spraying and he didn't want the Ovaro hit by their wild volleys. He left the horse, moved a half-dozen yards away and flattened himself on the ground beside the trunk of a big jack pine with the silence of a cougar on the prowl.

He peered out at the four men. They were frozen in place, watching for a movement, listening for any sound. Fargo saw the beads of perspiration rolling down their faces and decided to stay silent. They were already near the breaking point, small-time thugs with neither the experience, the training nor the inner steel to control their nerves. He let the seconds tick off, watching as the one with the slash across his face licked the dryness from his lips. He continued to stay silent as he saw the mounting nervousness seize the four men. With his rifle at his shoulder, Fargo remained beside the tree, almost smiling as he saw one of the four swallow hard, his hands trembling. It hadn't been much more than thirty seconds before one of them finally broke. It was the long-nosed one, but instead of making a move against his attacker, he caught Fargo by surprise by diving at the girl and making a shield out of her.

Fargo swung the big Henry, followed the diving figure and fired. The shot exploded just as the man reached the curled-up figure. Pitching forward, the diving figure landed half over the girl with a last shuddering gasp of breath. Fargo saw her uncurl and use her legs to kick the limp figure away from her. The other three fired a volley of shots into the trees. They sprayed the area and their bullets thudded into the trunk of the tree where Fargo hid. He stayed where he was, anticipating their next move. He heard their footsteps as they started to run away and he rolled out from behind the tree, watching them run to their horses. They were leaping into their saddles as Fargo rose on one knee, fired, and smiled as one of the trio flew from his horse. But the other two were racing away. Fargo rose, ran and vaulted onto the Ovaro.

He swerved the pinto between two pines and galloped after the fleeing riders, quickly glimpsing them as they tried to steer their horses through the dense forest. But their horses were as ordinary as they were and they had to slow down as they maneuvered their way through the denseness of the pines. The Ovaro, using its powerful jet-black hindquarters to cut in and out without losing any speed, closed the distance in minutes. Fargo raised the rifle to his shoulder again, took a moment to aim, waited for a clear shot, and fired, two shots echoing almost as one. Both the riders made strange, jerking motions as they fell from their horses and vanished in the brush. Fargo slowed the pinto, moved forward carefully and found both figures motionless in the high grass. He slowly turned the pinto around.

He made his way back to where the attack had begun and found the young woman on her feet, bending over one of the lifeless forms. She looked up as he appeared and swung down from the Ovaro. "I was going through their pockets, thought they might have something to identify them," she said with more calmness than he expected.

"Did they?" he asked, and she shook her head. She had taken off her hat, and he saw very deep, rich auburn hair that gave a new beauty to her face. The tan shirt tightened as she rose and he decided her breasts were perhaps not as modest as he'd first thought. "Whoever they were, they were definitely after you," Fargo said.

"How do you know that?" she asked.

"Overheard them talking last night. They had a description of you and an idea you'd be heading this way. They planned to get you. That's why I'm here," Fargo explained.

She stepped forward, extended a hand and he felt a firm grip. "Most would have gone their own way," she said.

"Thought about it," he smiled. "Couldn't shake off old habits."

"Thank God for that," she said. "You're an American."

"Bull's-eye."

"You got a name?"

"Fargo. . . . Skye Fargo. In the States, some call me the Trailsman." Her eyes widened.

"Really? It's a strange world. I've been looking for someone who can uncover a trail for me. In fact I've already spoken to a few men about the job," she said.

"Are you Heather Grandy?" Fargo queried.

"Yes," she said and ran one hand through the deep-auburn hair. "I wonder why they were after me."

"None of my business," Fargo shrugged.

"It will be if I hired you, Fargo." Heather Grandy smiled.

"I'm not here to work. I'm having myself a vacation," Fargo said. "I've never seen this part of your country."

"I'll make it more than worthwhile to skip your vacation," the young woman said, and her hand closed around his arm. "We have to talk more. How about tomorrow? I'm meeting with someone this afternoon."

"If it's somebody you're meeting for the job, I'd say hire him," Fargo remarked.

"No, it's a man whom I just met. He took a real fancy to me," Heather Grandy said.

"Can't blame him for that," Fargo said.

"Galantry in word as well as deed. You're an unusual

man, Fargo," she said. "Please think about letting me hire you?"

"I'll think about it, but no promises." He smiled, and suddenly her lips were on his, very soft and moist. Her kiss was a steady pressure that combined both pleasure and promise.

"That's to help you think," she murmured. "And for everything you did just now." When she pulled back, her hazel eyes had grown darker, a soft, simmering quality in their depths. She turned and pulled herself onto the dapple-grey. "I'm staying in the hotel in Lakeshore," she said. "I'll wait there for you." He watched her ride away with a great deal more composure than most young women would have displayed after barely avoiding a vicious attack. He waited until she was out of sight before climbing onto the pinto, passing the figures on the ground. Someone would find them sooner or later he thought as he moved on.

He was glad he'd followed old habits but he had certainly had his fill. He wanted to continue his vacation although he had to admit to himself that she was a very attractive young woman. Exploring this land with her might add another meaning to the word vacation. Still, all he wanted to do was to simply relax. He had broken trail for a large herd of Holsteins all the way from Kansas to Jim Mannion in upper Minnesota. He'd decided to go exploring the prairie province known as Rupert's Land, later called Manitoba.

Now he slowly continued his trip, taking in the feel of the land with its vast network of lakes and rivers. In some ways, it was not that different from the States, and in other ways, it had its own, special character. Even the names had their own feel to them, Dog Lake, Jackhead, Crane River, Reindeer Island, Dauphin, Neepawa, Wicked Point and so many others. They echoed the heritage of the land and nodded to the fierceness of the great Canadian winters. He had already seen moose and reindeer, but he knew the vast herds were still far to the north. It was summer and for the first time he felt like he was on vacation as he rode through vast fields of scarlet butterfly weed, wild bergamot, blue flag iris and purple loco, forests of white pine, jack pine, northern white cedar and juniper. The relaxed pleasures of the day began to draw to a close as he made his way back along the shore of Lake Winnipeg. He was nearing the hotel when he glimpsed Heather Grandy walking beside a slightly portly man in a tan frock coat and well-tailored trousers. Fargo saw a heavy face with thick, black hair and a flashy ring on one hand. He also saw the bulge of a holster under the frock coat.

As Heather walked on down the street with the man, Fargo rode the pinto to the stable, returned to the hotel and had a leisurely meal. He paused at the desk and asked the clerk about Heather Grandy, finding out she had the room adjoining his. After a nightcap of one more smooth Canadian whisky, he retired to his room, his body telling him he had ridden farther than he realized. He undressed, and idly made plans for moving northward via one of the flatboats that plied Lake Winnipeg. Finally, sleep wrapped itself around him and the little room grew silent.

He guessed a few hours had passed when sounds woke him. He pushed up on one elbow, and heard a man's voice raised in anger coming from the room next to him. A woman's voice answered and he instantly recognized it as Heather's, muffled as it was. He couldn't make out words but there was a sharpness in her tone. The man's voice came again, louder, demanding, then noises that sounded like a scuffle. Fargo had just swung his long legs over the edge of the narrow bed when he heard a single, popping sound, not really loud, not unlike the sound of a cork being pulled from a wine bottle. But it wasn't a cork. He knew that sound. It was the unmistakable sound of a derringer going off. He frowned into the dark, frozen for a moment, and then another sound exploded, loud and deep. This was the instantly recognizable sound of a big-bore revolver.

Leaping from his bed, he pulled on trousers and strapped on his gun belt as he dashed from the room. He was at the door of the adjoining room in seconds, turning the knob and swinging the door wide open. He burst in, Colt in hand. Heather Grandy turned as he came in, her eyes wide; she was looking lovely in an emerald-green dress with a deep V neckline. He tore his eyes from the soft swell of her cleavage, and brought them to the figure on the floor. It was the man he had seen with her earlier in the day, only now he was lying on his back, very dead, with a circular stain spreading across his silk shirt. Fargo saw the revolver on the floor, a big .44-caliber Remington Army revolver with an eight-inch barrel. Heather flew to him and wrapped her arms around him.

"He was going to rape me," she gasped. "He was starting to do it and he wouldn't stop." Fargo half turned at the sound behind him. The desk clerk stood in the doorway, staring down at the lifeless figure.

"My God," he breathed. "I'm getting the sheriff." Spinning, he raced away down the hall. Fargo turned back to Heather Grandy as she clung to his arm.

"He pinned me on the bed. He wouldn't listen to me, wouldn't stop," she said. "I saw the gun and pulled it from his holster. He grabbed at it and we fought. It was either that or let him rape me, and I wasn't about to do that." She halted, peered at Fargo. "Where were you? How'd you get here so fast?" she asked.

"In the next room," he said and she leaned her head on his chest.

"It seems you know when I need you. I'm glad for that," Heather murmured, and he felt the soft swell of her breasts against him. He held her but his eyes narrowed in thought. He had no reason not to accept the story as she told it to him. It was a chain of events that happened all the time, an unfortunate pattern in the relationships of some men and women. But she hadn't told him all of it. The sound of the derringer stuck in his mind. She hadn't mentioned that, and he frowned. He wasn't one for imagining sounds. He was about to ask her about it when he heard footsteps coming down the hall. Heather stepped back as the desk clerk entered with a man wearing a sheriff's badge and another with a deputy's shield. The sheriff, a square-faced man with salt-and-pepper hair, stared down at the man on the floor.

"Ernie Binder," he grunted.

"You know him?" Heather said.

"Local gambler. Big man with dice and dames," the sheriff said. "I'm Sheriff Greavy."

"Heather Grandy. I've been staying here at the hotel," Heather said.

"You kill him?" Sheriff Greavy asked.

"I'm afraid so. I had to," Heather replied.

"You want to fill me in?" the sheriff said.

"I met him a few days ago. He was very attentive. We spent the evening dining and drinking, but when he brought me back here he tried to force himself on me. I didn't expect that," Heather said.

"You that innocent?" the sheriff tossed at her.

Fargo saw her hazel eyes flare. "I guess so," she snapped and proceeded to tell the sheriff the details she had told Fargo. When she finished, the sheriff pursed his lips.

"It's not a new story. You just made it turn out differently than it usually does," he said.

"I'd rather my way than his," Heather said.

"I don't disbelieve you, but it's just your word. He's not talking," the sheriff said. "I like something more than just somebody's word."

"How about common sense, the look of things, logic?"

Heather returned. "I told you what happened. I grabbed his gun to defend myself. I don't carry a big six-gun."

The sheriff knelt down to the man and searched through his pockets, drawing out some change and a few pound notes. "Ernie always carried a big roll of American dollars, at least a thousand if not more. He called it his 'on-the-spot bankroll.' It's not here," Greavy said.

"Are you saying I robbed him?" Heather frowned. "Feel free to search my things. I shot him to stop him from raping me. That's what it was, nothing else."

The sheriff turned to Fargo. "Who are you and where do you fit in here, mister?" he asked.

"Name's Skye Fargo. I'm in the room next door. I heard the noise, then the shot, and came to see," Fargo said.

"Really now? Way I see it, you could've shot him, over her, maybe. I want more than words," Greavy said.

"Seems that's what you'll have to go with, hers and mine," Fargo said.

"Not completely," the sheriff said and turned to the desk clerk. "Get Doc Hawthorn," he said, and the clerk hurried away. He ran to the saloon next door and returned minutes later with a tall, thin man carrying a black doctor's bag. He wore horn-rimmed glasses that sat on a thin, straight nose. Fargo instantly smelled the scent of alcohol on him. The doctor glanced down at the man on the floor.

"Ernie Binder?" he said.

"Himself," Greavy grunted. "We'll take him to your place. You'll get me something besides words, something like a bullet." He turned to Fargo. "You're carrying a Colt. If the bullet the doc takes out of Ernie Binder is from a Colt, you're in trouble, mister. If it's a forty-four caliber from a Remington, you're in the clear. So's the lady. It'll back up her story on using his own gun on him."

"Fair enough," Fargo said. As the sheriff's deputy and

the desk clerk carried Ernie Binder from the room, Sheriff Greavy turned to Heather.

"Stay in the hotel till we get back to you," he said. "Same for you, Fargo." He strode from the room and Fargo met Heather's eyes.

"Thanks for being here," she said. "I knew it wouldn't go easily. Sheriffs never take a woman's word on its own."

"I'll get dressed," Fargo said. "It could be a long wait."

"I hope the doctor finds the bullet. We're both in trouble if he doesn't," Heather said.

"Why wouldn't he?" Fargo questioned.

"I don't know." Heather shrugged. "Maybe it's not in him. Maybe it went clear through him."

"Then it ought to be on the floor here someplace. Let's have a look," Fargo said and started to move slowly across one side of the room. Heather took the other side and joined him as he ended his search peering under the bed. No bullet turned up, and Fargo pushed to his feet. "Guess we wait for what the doc finds," he said. "I'll see you later."

He turned and walked to the door, saw her watching him. She had the same calm manner as she had after the six men tried to attack her. He wondered if it was self-discipline or part of her nature. Whichever it was, not many young women had it, he commented silently. Reaching his room, he closed the door, dressed, and stretched out on the bed. He found himself frowning into space as his thoughts kept returning to the sound of the derringer. Heather hadn't mentioned a derringer to the sheriff, either. Yet he was sure he had heard the sound of the gun, Fargo told himself as his lips thinned. Could he be certain of what he'd heard? The question danced in his mind. It had happened moments after he'd wakened. Had he heard something else? Dammit, he swore angrily. The derringer made a distinctive sound

and he didn't go for imagining things. His lips stayed
tight as he swore to himself he'd find out the truth. It
had become a question he'd not carry around with him
unanswered, he decided as he closed his eyes to wait.
Either way it was quite clear to him that his vacation
was over.

Jason Manning

❏ **Mountain Passage**   0-451-19569-8/$5.99
Leaving Ireland for the shores of America, a young man loses his parents
en route—one to death, one to insanity—and falls victim to the sadistic
captain of the ship. Luckily, he is befriended by a legendary Scottish
adventurer, whom he accompanies to the wild American frontier. But
along the way, new troubles await....

❏ **Mountain Massacre**   0-451-19689-9/$5.99
Receiving word that his mother has passed away, mountain man Gordon
Hawkes reluctantly returns home to Missouri to pick up the package she
left for him. Upon arrival, he is attacked by a posse looking to collect the
bounty on his head. In order to escape, Hawkes decides to hide out among
the Mormons and guide them to their own promised land. But the trek
turns deadly when the religious order splits into two factions...with
Hawkes caught in the middle!

❏ **Mountain Courage**   0-451-19870-0/$5.99
Gordon Hawkes' hard-won peace and prosperity are about to be threatened by the bloody clouds of war. While Gordon is escorting the Crow
tribe's yearly annuity from the U.S. government, the Sioux ambush the
shipment. Captured, Gordon must decide whether to live as a slave, die as
a prisoner, or renounce his life and join the Sioux tribe. His only hope is
his son Cameron, who must fight his father's captors and bring Hawkes
back alive.